RANDOM ACTS
OF FRAUD

A Holly Anna Paladin Mystery,
Book 5

By Christy Barritt

RANDOM ACTS OF FRAUD

Random Acts of Fraud: A Novel
Copyright 2017 by Christy Barritt

Published by River Heights Press

Cover design by The Killion Group

RANDOM ACTS OF FRAUD

CHAPTER 1

I glanced around the busy city street, one that bustled with throngs of twentysomethings indulging in Saturday evening nightlife in downtown Cincinnati. Numerous hotspot restaurants and clubs claimed the area, and most of the people traversing these streets tonight seemed content to bounce from one location to another, following whatever whim seemed appealing or popular.

The scent around me defined this whole experience. It was either body odor from the crowd or sewer gases, but the two blended into one in my mind, creating an unalluring, totally regrettable experience that summed up the last ten minutes.

My best friend, Jamie Duke, had convinced me to sign up for an online dating service in order to overcome the romantic slump I'd been in since I'd ended my engagement three months ago. Meeting potential dates via the web was horrible on so many levels. And now I was standing on the sidewalk with Jamie as we waited for our dates to arrive. This was like waiting for a tetanus shot and knowing how much it was going to hurt.

I shoved my hands deep into the pockets of my jean jacket, feeling like a crusty senior citizen attending a wild and crazy rave. The vibe emanating from others was energetic and fun. The vibe around *me* was etched with grumpiness and apprehension.

I was twenty-nine, far from a senior citizen. I might as well be, however. I related to people well into their seventies and eighties more than I did people in my own age group. I liked old-timey values and front porches and face-to-face conversations. I did not like online dating. I didn't like anything about it. And I did not like being here right now.

"I'm going home," I announced to Jamie. Then another realization stopped me cold. "But that would be rude."

"That's right, girl. It *would* be rude." She crossed her arms and pursed her lips. Classic Jamie.

My friend had a distinct style and personality of her own, one that was often defined by the black curly hair that bounced from her face in a modern-day, ultra-stylish Afro. Her skin was light brown and her body curvy in the right places, especially now that she'd lost more than a hundred pounds and turned her life around through exercise and eating right.

Her expression showed pure stubbornness. She wouldn't let me get out of this easily. That meant I needed a good, solid argument, one that would be sure to justify an early departure.

"Audrey Hepburn would have never done this," I finally said.

"I know she's a role model of sorts to you, but who

knows what modern-day Hollywood would have done to her in this day and age. She very well could be out fighting for every woman's right to have hairy armpits."

I gasped, the very idea appalling on so many different levels. So. Many. Levels. "Take it back."

"Nope, not going to do it." Jamie looked like she might continue bursting my bubble, but then she perked as her gaze zeroed in on someone in the distance. "Oh look, there's Luke. He looks . . . different . . . from his profile picture."

I observed the guy. He was tall—really tall—and thin. He walked like a basketball star, his bounce-like cadence seeming to match a player leisurely dribbling a ball down the court. As soon as I saw the massive gold chain around his neck and the matching bling on his teeth, I knew exactly how this evening would turn out.

His gaze zeroed on Jamie, and he nodded an aloof greeting.

"You must be Jamie." He stopped in front of us, giving off a definite "I'm full of myself" vibe.

Jamie and Luke exchanged a few lines of dialogue, which I tried to tune out. This was all a bad, bad idea. I could try to justify it all I wanted, but the truth was the truth.

I wasn't ready to date again.

I drew in a deep breath and glanced down the street, trying to give the two their moment. They were never going to make it. If only I could sense for myself the things that I could sense so easily in others.

Just then, someone rammed into me, nearly knocking me off my feet and snapping me back to reality.

I gasped as a man grabbed my shoulders, catching me before I tumbled onto the sidewalk. His gaze darted around wildly, and adrenaline pumped from his sweat-laden skin.

"Sorry," he muttered, dragging in a ragged breath. He glanced at me, and something flashed in his eyes. Was that recognition? "Be careful."

As quickly as he appeared, he was gone. He rushed down the street, urgency charging his every movement. People nowadays. They were in such a hurry all the time.

"Are you okay?" Jamie asked.

I nodded, still startled by the stranger's hit-and-run. "Yeah. I mean, yes." Where was my etiquette? "I'm fine. Thank you."

"Some people are so rude," Jamie muttered with pursed lips. "Like me. I haven't introduced you yet. Holly, this is Luke. Luke, Holly."

I forced a smile, wanting to be anywhere but here. Had I mentioned that yet?

"It's so nice to meet you," I said anyway.

"You too," Luke said. Nothing about his words sounded sincere.

I glanced around, still feeling self-conscious. My own date was ten minutes late. Which was unacceptable. Late people drove me *crazy*.

But Jamie and I had agreed to only double date. We both knew firsthand that there were too many crazies out there to go on these rendezvous alone. If my online date didn't show up, I couldn't leave Jamie alone with

Luke. I would be relegated to third wheel.

My night just got a thousand times worse.

"Let's give Travis five more minutes," Jamie said, seeming to read both my thoughts and my unease.

"I think we've given him plenty of time," I said. "We should go eat. You guys can just pretend like I'm not there. I will practically be invisible, I assure you."

Luke shifted, as if he didn't know what to say. He was probably hoping I would bow out. That was what most normal people would hope for. But a promise was a promise. I couldn't leave Jamie.

"If you'd brought your cell phone, you could check to see if he texted about being late," Jamie said, a vaguely scolding tone to her voice.

"It really bugs me when people stare at their phones during a conversation instead of looking at the person speaking with them," I explained to her again. "To avoid that happening, I simply left my phone at home."

"Well, that might be a non-issue right now. It will be hard for him to be glued to his own phone while with you if he doesn't even show up."

Before Jamie could object, I turned on my heel and started toward the restaurant down the street. Luke had claimed he didn't know where the restaurant was, so we'd agreed to meet at a more central location near Fountain Square. As I rounded the corner, I stopped so quickly that Jamie nearly collided into me.

"What on God's green earth are you doing, girl?" she asked.

I pointed to the Mustang parked on the street and muttered, "That's Travis's car."

I was a Mustang enthusiast, and that was one of the reasons I'd agreed to go out with this guy. We both loved the vehicle. He'd sent me pictures of his car even. It was a cherry-red '66 Mustang.

"Are you sure that's his?" A wrinkle formed between Jamie's eyes as she stared across the street.

My cheeks heated as I nodded. "His has that navy blue pinstripe on the bottom. It's custom. He mentioned that."

Even worse than seeing his car, I could see Travis Strongman sitting inside the car. He wasn't moving. Maybe he'd seen me, had gotten cold feet, and was now contemplating how to get out of this date. Even though I could relate to the getting cold feet part, it was still insulting.

Jamie threw her shoulders back and let out a harrumph. "He can't stand you up. I'm going to give him a piece of my mind."

I grabbed her arm before she could charge toward the car and do something to further add injury to insult. "You don't have to do that, Jamie. It's better to cut my losses now rather than later."

My cheeks warmed, and my body desperately sought a rock to hide under. Since there were no rocks here on the city street, I'd settle for a mailbox or newspaper stand. Anything. Maybe even a phone booth where I could magically transform into someone else. A superhero with invisibility as her super power.

"Of course, I do. This is unacceptable." Her voice rose with her signature urban sass, and I could tell "the diva" might emerge at any minute. "The diva" was how I described one of Jamie's idiosyncrasies. When she got fired up about something, every bit of feistiness rose in her, usually ending with a Z-shaped finger snap, jutted hips, and dramatically pursed lips.

I stepped closer, lowering my voice even more so Luke wouldn't hear my confession. "What if he saw me and changed his mind?"

Jamie scoffed and pulled her head back until an uncustomary double chin appeared. "That's ridiculous. You're gorgeous. Why would he change his mind?"

I didn't really want to explain this to her. It was humiliating. "Because the dating game is cruel," I whispered. "I'm not cut out for this. I like doing things the traditional way."

Panic—and a good dose of insecurity—rose in me. Put me in a social work situation, and I was golden. In my element. I could bring cookies to shut-ins, visit the chronically ill in the hospital, or host a party like a pro.

But dating? That was an entirely different story.

Jamie paused and squeezed my hand. "I'm sorry I pushed you into this, Holly. But this guy is not going to get away with standing you up. He needs to man up. There are a shortage of real men around here, and it's a crying shame that people think they can treat others this way."

That uncomfortable feeling squeezed my gut again. I hated when people made scenes. I *really* hated it when I was the cause of that scene. It was so unbecoming.

But once Jamie got something in her mind, there was no changing it. I just had to brace myself for the gale-force winds that came with Hurricane Jamie. Her sunshine quickly turned into the blinding glare of a nuclear explosion.

As she charged toward the Mustang, I glanced at Luke and smiled apologetically.

"She's a spitfire, isn't she?" Luke said, a touch of admiration staining his otherwise aloof gaze as he stared after Jamie.

"She is. She's the person you want on your side when things go south. Devoted to a fault."

"That's good to know. I'm into loyalty and spunk."

"Then you should love Jamie." I braced myself as my friend reached the car door and pounded on the window.

I waited, holding my breath as I anticipated what might play out next. Nothing happened.

Travis didn't move. I could still see his silhouette in the driver's seat. What was his problem?

Jamie's hand went to her hip as she waited impatiently for a response. Then she rapped at the window again. Tapped her foot. Gave Travis a death stare. I couldn't see her face, but I knew her well enough to know that I didn't have to see her expression to know the stare was there.

This was painful. So painful.

"Jamie, we should just go—" I called, looking for that mailbox to disappear beneath.

"This guy is not getting away with being a jerk." Jamie grabbed the door handle.

Horror washed through me. I stepped forward to stop her and end this madness before it got out of control.

As I did, Jamie jerked the door open. She opened her mouth to give the man a verbal lashing when the man's silhouette abruptly shifted.

He slumped and fell onto the street.

Jamie lurched backward.

I couldn't believe my eyes.

Based on the pallor of the man's skin and his motionless body, it appeared Travis Strongman was dead.

CHAPTER 2

Of all the detectives that would show up at the scene, of course Chase Dexter just happened to be working tonight. That was just . . . lovely. A way to make a humiliating night even more humiliating.

As soon as I saw my ex-boyfriend striding my way across the sidewalk, my cheeks flushed. A hollow feeling swelled inside my stomach, like a balloon filled to capacity and about to burst.

When would I stop reacting to Chase like this? How would I ever forget the year we'd dated? How much I loved him? How impossible a future together would be?

His gaze was like a laser beam on me as he approached. I'd been largely avoiding him for the past three months. Occasionally, we'd text or run into each other. But it was better if we didn't speak because, when we did, I just wanted to forget about my convictions and run back into his familiar, strong arms.

Chase didn't look at the crime scene or the officers surrounding it or the crowds that had gathered. No, his eyes were solely on me. Concern, curiosity, and . . . something else . . . lingered in the depths of his baby blues.

He squeezed my arm and stooped slightly to meet me eye to eye. "Holly . . . I didn't realize you'd be here. Are you okay?"

I nodded, my arms still crossed over my chest and a hand halfway covering my gaping mouth. "Yes, I'm fine. I'm better than that guy."

His gaze lingered on me one more minute—inquisitive and probing—until he glanced over at the car. Yellow crime-scene tape had been strung around the area and patrol officers surrounded it, trying to keep away gawkers.

It had been a circus around here since Travis fell from the car. Some people had run away screaming. Others had been desperate for a glimpse of what was happening. Others had their phones raised and their fingers sprinted across the screen in a race to break the news on social media. They acted like he wasn't someone's son or friend or coworker. Like he wasn't a person but a news story or a clip from their favorite TV show.

And that was what was wrong with our society today. Compassion had been replaced with the desire for attention. Tragedy was a means to achieve social media buzz.

Jamie and I had done our best to secure the scene until the police arrived. It was the least we could do.

Yes, the least I could do.

I somehow felt responsible for this. Which was stupid. And I knew that. But I felt that way nonetheless.

"How did you know this guy?" Chase's voice sounded tight and slightly edgy as he turned back to me.

The orange glow from an overhead sign illuminated part of his face—a face of which I'd studied every inch. That I'd caressed. That I'd wanted to wake up to each morning.

Focus, Holly. Focus.

I moved my hand from my mouth and rubbed my throat instead. "I didn't know him. Not really. We'd communicated a few times via email and texts."

Chase continued to study me, almost as if no one else was near, even though everything was churning and spinning around us at a maddening pace yet painfully slow at the same time.

"What does that mean?" He tilted his head.

"It was me." Jamie stepped into our conversation and relieved me of all the uncomfortable things I'd been on the verge of saying. "I convinced Holly to try this new online dating site. Winkable.com. All of this was my idea. She was supposed to meet this guy tonight, and this is how we found him."

Was that disappointment in Chase's gaze? Jealousy? I wasn't sure.

Nor was I sure why I felt guilty. Chase and I had broken up. We were free to do whatever we wanted with whomever we wanted whenever we wanted. Which sounded way more promiscuous than it actually was.

I squeezed the skin between my eyes. My emotions panged all over the place tonight, and I just wanted to go home and enjoy some peace and quiet while listening to Frank Sinatra. Maybe even take up knitting and crossword puzzles. Buy a cat. Or ten.

Chase straightened, seeming colder and more distant with every passing minute. "His name?"

"Travis Strongman." My throat ached with the words. "He's doing his medical residency at Good Samaritan."

"Know anything else about him?" He held a notepad and pen in hand, scribbling notes and snapping into professional mode.

"Not really," I said. "He likes mountain biking and vacationing at the beach. He's a car enthusiast, and he wants to help children with life-threatening illnesses."

Chase nodded slowly and wrote something else on that pad of paper. "I'm going to need you to hang around, Holly. You too, Jamie."

"Of course," we both said at the same time.

As soon as he walked back toward the Mustang, I turned to Jamie. My stomach roiled as everything flashed back to me.

Please don't let me throw up. It would only serve to humiliate me more, and I've had enough of that tonight.

It was just the two of us now. Too-cool Luke had said he was going to get coffee for us. That was twenty minutes ago. I didn't think he'd be returning. Go figure. A person's strength could be determined not by how they reacted to the good times in life but to the hard times. My dad had often said that. He may have been a blue-collar worker, but he'd had the wisdom of a philosopher.

"Could you tell how he died?" I whispered to Jamie, some of my shock wearing off and my wheels starting to turn.

Jamie shook her head and pulled her shawl tighter around her shoulders. "No, I couldn't. I didn't see any blood."

I rubbed my arms, staring at the sea of onlookers. Was the killer here? Had he come back to watch the crowd react to what he'd done? I scanned the faces around me, but none looked suspicious.

"Why does stuff like this always happen to us?" I muttered, replaying all the mysteries and adventures Jamie and I had somehow been involved with in the past.

"That's a great question. Last time, it was an abandoned baby. The time before that . . . well, it was your fault."

It couldn't argue. It had been my fault. I'd been concerned about Chase, so I'd followed him to Louisville. It wasn't my proudest moment. In fact, it had been slightly stalkerish. But I'd had good intentions. I promise.

"The time before that it was because a psycho provoked you to do his bidding."

"Psychos like to provoke me apparently."

"And then, the time before *that,* it was because you decided to break into people's homes in order to clean them and brighten their day."

I frowned. "Also not one of my brightest ideas. Especially when it's said aloud and without explanation."

"I'm not really sure how I let you talk me into these things."

"The good news is that we have no personal

connection to this case," I said, trying to look on the bright side. "I mean, as far as we can tell, right? So, after we're done here today, we should be done. No investigating or getting involved or running for our lives."

"That's right. Those days are behind us, girlfriend. They're as gone as WKRP." She paused before singing, "in Cincinnati."

I nodded, wishing I felt as convinced as I sounded.

I shivered and glanced around. The crowds remained. Patrol officers tried to control the scene. A traffic light changed to green above us.

None of those things answered the question that had rammed into my mind. Why did I feel like someone was watching me as I stood here on the sidewalk? Like I had a spotlight on me, alerting everyone that I was vaguely connected to this?

I also had the feeling that this wasn't over, despite what I'd said to Jamie. I'd been trying to convince myself, just as much as Jamie.

Was this some sort of purgatory for my sin of online dating? That's what it felt like.

Dear Lord, help this be over, and I promise I won't ever try online dating again. Never. Ever.

***

Two hours later, I was at the police precinct. Chase had more questions for Jamie and me, and he preferred we come into the station where it was more private.

And I felt awkward. Again.

A classy woman was graceful. That was what I was aiming for—to act like a lady, despite living in a society that applauded unladylike behavior. Instead, I felt self-conscious and obstinate at the moment and like the opposite of whom I wanted to be.

I didn't want to feel this way around Chase. But I did. My well-used *Book of Manners* didn't exactly tell me how I should handle this situation.

After all, my life could be the punch line of a bad joke right now. *A murderer, an ex-boyfriend, and a blind date walked into a bar . . .*

I shifted nervously in the padded chair across from Chase's desk and glanced around his office. I'd been in here many times before. I remembered sharing quick lunches, exchanging lovelorn glances, feeling the charge between us as we bonded over investigations. Over justice. That's what it was all about for me. I wanted to be a voice for the voiceless.

There was a blank area on his desk where a picture of the two of us used to be. It was gone, a stark reminder of what had been but was no longer. My throat clinched at the thought.

Jamie sat in the chair next to me, texting an update to her family. If I had my phone with me, I might text my own mother, but she was out of town at a real estate conference in Florida.

As I sat there, legs crossed at the ankles and my head straight enough to balance a book on, my thoughts drifted back to Travis. Every time I closed my eyes, I could picture him tumbling from his car and onto the street. I could visualize his lifeless eyes. I could feel the despair that death caused.

I shivered.

Now that my brain fog had cleared, questions raced at a frightening speed through my mind. How had Travis died? When? Most importantly, why?

Finally, Chase came into his office and sat across from us. His presence filled the entire room—as did his person. Chase was six feet three inches, as broad and thick as Thor, and he had a personality to match. He'd played professional football for a few years before an injury sidelined him and ultimately led him to turn his life around from self-serving playboy to community-minded detective.

I held my breath as I waited for what he had to say. I dreaded the disappointment I might see in his eyes. I felt a well of loss at how our relationship had been transformed into this stiff, uncomfortable menagerie of emotions that twisted my thoughts and heart.

"Well, there's good news and bad news." Chase's gaze darted back and forth between me and Jamie. "I'll start with the bad news. According to his driver's license, Travis Strongman wasn't that man's real name."

My mouth gaped open. The man had clearly listed his name on his online profile as Travis Strongman. I hadn't even considered that he'd fake that.

"Really?" I asked. "Why would he lie about his name?"

"Welcome to the world of online dating." Chase's jaw flexed again.

He didn't like the fact that I was trying to move on, did he? Yet he had the power to change our relationship

21

status. However, he insisted he couldn't.

And that was that.

I shoved those thoughts aside and cleared my throat. "What's the good news?"

"The good news is that you didn't physically interact with this guy, who was not whom he presented himself as. We don't know his true identity yet, but we're bringing in the owner of the car to see if he can shed some light on things."

"He didn't even own that car?" I blinked, honestly stunned. "How . . . inconsiderate."

I'd been scammed. I'd thought I was smarter than that. But I was a fool for love, just like so many other single gals out there.

Jamie threw me a compassionate look and gripped her phone, as if waiting for a return text.

"No, the car belongs to someone named Drew Williams."

I leaned back, still reeling from everything I was learning. I expected guys to exaggerate how much money they made, just like women underestimated how much they weighed. But not this.

"I never expected this level of deceit," I finally said.

Chase's heated gaze lingered on mine again. I knew him well enough to know that he was struggling with how to respond. He'd always been protective of me. And we had a great friendship. These were new waters to traverse between us, and, the sooner we learned how to navigate them, the better.

We went over everything I knew about Travis, which wasn't much. I'd begun chatting with him two weeks ago. He'd seen my picture on the site, and he'd winked at me. That was how it all started on Winkable.com. Our online conversation had continued for much longer than most of the people I'd connected with there.

Travis whatever-his-real-name-was had seemed nice enough. He was thirty-one—two years older than I was. As far as I knew—if he'd been telling the truth— he'd never been married and didn't have any kids. Now that I thought about it, we hadn't gone very deep in our conversations. He'd actually asked a lot of questions about me, which was a bit of a role reversal.

I was usually the one probing for more information about other people. I'd discovered early in life that people loved to talk about themselves and that most people craved someone who truly listened. I liked playing the role of nurturer.

"May I ask how he died?" My hands trembled in my lap as I asked the question. I had too much experience with death and murder and grief. It never got easier. And I never wanted it to. Struggling with those things made me human.

Chase's hard gaze met mine again, his blue eyes full of questions. "We don't know for sure. The medical examiner will give the final verdict. There was a small puncture mark on his neck, however."

My blood cooled even more.

"You were both standing close by," Chase continued, tapping his pen against the desk. "Did you see anything unusual in the moments before you discovered he was dead?"

"We were actually around the corner before we stumbled upon Travis," Jamie said. "The car was out of sight for the majority of time we were waiting. We didn't spot it until we started toward the restaurant."

"So, you never rode with him?" Chase clarified, his gaze wandering to mine again.

"No, of course not," I said. "We agreed to meet outside the restaurant."

"That's good. If you're going to date strangers you meet online, please don't let them know where you live."

A flash of irritation jolted through me. Chase had no right to dictate what I did in my dating life. He'd lost that privilege. Nor should he treat me like I was naïve. I was smarter than that. People often mistook my kindness for weakness, and it made me want to do something . . . something . . . something very unkind.

Chase let out a long breath. "Is there anything else that stands out to either of you?"

I started to shake my head, simply ready to get out of here. Before I could complete that thought, Jamie jolted into an upright position, and she snapped her fingers.

"That man who ran into you!" Jamie turned toward me, excitement lighting her eyes.

That was right! I'd forgotten about the man who'd nearly pushed me down on the sidewalk. But could he possibly be connected with this? It seemed like a long shot.

"He seemed in a hurry," I said. "Or like he was being chased. I didn't think terribly much of it. You know how people can be sometimes. They're especially brisk downtown. And he told me to be careful."

"To be careful?" Chase raised an eyebrow.

"I thought it was strange, but everything happened so fast."

"Can you describe him?" Chased shifted in his seat and pulled out that pad of paper again.

I recalled our encounter. How the man's hands had gripped my arms. How he'd muttered he was sorry while glancing around. How he'd never made eye contact. "Sure. He was Caucasian, probably in his early thirties, and he had a thin build. He had dark hair, a thin beard—"

"Thin how?" Chase asked.

"Thin as in it just skimmed the edges of his jaw, like an outline," I explained. "I'm sure there's a better word for it."

"I believe it's called a chinstrap beard," Jamie chirped.

"Chinstrap beard it is." He nodded. "Keep going."

"He was probably five inches taller than I," I continued. "Five ten maybe? He had a lean build. Light eyes. Maybe green. Possibly hazel. I'm not sure—it was dark outside."

"Anything else you noticed?"

I closed my eyes and remembered the scene again. What was I missing? There was something else at the edge of my remembrance, begging for me to share it. "He smelled like curry."

Chase raised an eyebrow. "I wasn't expecting that one."

I nodded, a surprising surge of excitement rushing through me. "It's a pretty noticeable odor. Maybe he'd just eaten Indian food somewhere? I know there are a couple of restaurants downtown."

"We'll look into it. Good detail."

A knock sounded outside Chase's office. As my head swiveled toward the noise, I spotted a man standing in the open doorway. He was probably my age, maybe a little older. He had black hair, classic features, and a certain warmth exuded from him.

"Detective Dexter?" he said.

Chase rose. "Yes?"

"I'm Drew. Drew Williams." He extended his hand and smiled, but the action was almost apologetic. "The Mustang's owner."

"Thanks for coming," Chase said. "I have some questions for you."

"Of course. Anything I can do." Drew's gaze flickered over to Jamie and then me. He paused, and his gaze latched onto mine. Uncertainty fluttered in the depths of his deep browns. "Have we met before?"

I smoothed my skirt, squirming under his scrutiny. "I don't think so."

I'd remember someone who looked like Drew Williams. At first glance, he struck me as the type who'd break out tap dancing on the city streets while holding an umbrella for his woman like in one of those old movies. Something about him screamed "gentleman."

I stood, knowing I couldn't be here for Chase's conversation with Drew, even though I longed for some answers. Unanswered questions drove me mad, and they were likely to be the death of me one day. It was like leaving a wall half-painted or a cake unfrosted.

Drew continued to study me with unapologetic curiosity, one hand casually stuffed into his pocket. "You go to Community Church, don't you?"

Surprise washed through me—half curious surprise and half cautious surprise. "I do."

A satisfied look replaced his uncertainty. "I've seen you there. You sing in the choir."

My cheeks warmed. It was a large choir—seventy-five people. Not the kind I usually got noticed for being a part of. "Guilty as charged. Mezzo soprano. Second row on the right. Beside Gladys who has bright red hair styled in a beehive."

A grin cracked his face. "Yes, you stand out on stage. I couldn't help but notice you. You're like an angel up there."

My cheeks warmed even more. This was all flattering . . . but awkward. Chase stood between us, listening to every word of our conversation.

"Thank you . . . I think." I nodded at Chase, wishing I could catch my breath and gather my thoughts and maybe even make some cookies. Cookies always made everything better. "I should go now."

Drew made no effort to move and let me through the doorway. "Listen, I know this is unusual and kind of forward, but I'm not sure when I'll get the opportunity again. I'm having a Bible study at my place on Monday evening. Come."

My thoughts flatlined. "Um . . . I'll need to check my schedule."

"Do that. But I hope it works out. Call me at Wilford Funeral Home, and I'll give you my address."

"What?" Why would I call him at a funeral home? Had I misunderstood something?

He smiled again, flashing white perfect teeth. "I know it sounds strange. But I own the place. My assistant can track me down there. Otherwise, I can call you back once my duties are done."

"I'll think about it," I finally said.

I glanced back at Chase, unsure what he was thinking right now. Even though the man was just asking me to a Bible study, the whole exchange felt a little strange. Of course, Drew probably had no idea what my history with Chase was. To him, Chase was just the detective on the case.

Drew stepped out of the way, and I started through the door, catching a quick whiff of sandalwood cologne. Before I could flee the scene, Chase called out to me.

"Holly?"

I pivoted toward him, and our gazes caught. "Yes?"

"Could you wait around a few minutes? I'll give you a ride home if Jamie needs to go."

My head started pounding. Why did this feel so complicated? "Sure. I'll wait."

Those cookies would have to be delayed until a little later. Right now, I had to prepare myself to work with Chase, even if it was just momentarily. And I somehow needed to do it without letting on just how catastrophically he'd crushed my heart.

CHAPTER 3

As soon as the door to Chase's office was closed, I released my breath, finally feeling like I could breathe now that I was away from Chase—and Drew.

"You want me to wait?" Jamie asked, her car keys dangling in her hands. "You head-turning, angelic-looking, choir-singing woman."

I slapped her arm. "Oh, stop."

"I'm the only one who sings onstage at my church, and no one notices me."

"That's not true. Everyone loves you."

"Hm hm." She sounded doubtful. "Now, back to my question. Wait or go?"

"Why don't you go ahead? I'll be okay." I knew she had a busy day tomorrow. She was leading worship at church, and then they were having a luncheon afterward. She was in charge of both.

"You sure?" She scrunched her eyes and studied my face like only a BFF could.

I plastered on a smile, trying to make her feel better, even though a tornado still spun inside me. "Yes, I'm sure."

She made no move to leave. Instead, she leaned closer and lowered her voice. "That Drew guy is pretty cute."

"I suppose. I had other things on my mind." Okay, I'd totally noticed, but I felt guilty admitting it.

"Understandably. But maybe this was all fortuitous."

Her words stopped my thoughts in their emotionally fraught tracks. "What do you mean?"

She shrugged and switched gears, not hiding the mischievous sparkle in her eyes. "Nothing. Okay, if you'd like to stay, I need to compose a nasty gram to Luke. I can't believe he didn't come back. Dating is for the birds."

"There's always Wesley."

She raised her chin. "He's out of the picture for now."

"But he will return to this area, and I really think he's open to seeing you again."

Wesley had seemed perfect for Jamie. He owned an IT company, and he was a triathlete. But he'd left for a cross-country bike trip to raise money for PTSD victims, and the two had decided to take a break since their relationship was so brand spanking new when he'd had to leave. She'd been happy for a whole three weeks prior to that.

After Jamie left the station, I leaned against the wall outside Chase's door and called hello to some of the officers I knew as they passed. Several stopped to chat for a few minutes, but a few gave me the cold shoulder. What was that about?

As a social worker, I'd worked with many of the department's finest.

In fact, Chase and I had reconnected several years ago because of my social work and his police work. We'd gone to high school together, but I'd thought he hated me. Truth was, I'd had a crush on him for a long time before we'd actually dated. Our paths had gone separate ways until finally tangling again a little more than a year ago.

He'd been a dream come true.

And then I'd woken up, and what we'd had was gone.

Voices drifted through the door behind me.

"That's my car," Drew said. "I let Travis borrow it. Travis Hooker."

Hooker? No wonder the man had made up a last name—an extremely masculine last name like Strongman. What kind of man—or woman—wanted to be a part of the Hooker family?

"How did you know Travis?" Chase asked.

"He worked for me," Drew said. "Not directly, I should clarify. But I hire the company he works for, Dillow Mortuary Transportation, so I've interacted with him many times. Enough that he was comfortable enough asking to borrow my car for a date. I had no idea he was telling people the vehicle was his."

"What else can you tell me about Travis?" Chase asked.

"He seemed to be a good employee. He was always on time. I had no complaints about him."

"Did anyone have any problems with him?"

Silence lingered a moment. Then, "I think he was having some trouble with his boss, Ronald. Honestly, I didn't get into it. I didn't want to know unless it involved me."

"None of your clients complained about him either?"

"Now that you mention it, there was one family three or four months ago who didn't like him. But the man was in the throes of grief. His wife had just died because a drunk driver hit her. He seemed to be taking out a lot of his anger on Travis. That happens sometimes."

"Do you remember his name?"

"I can find it for you when I get back to the office."

I couldn't make out the rest of their conversation. And I'd secretly wanted to make it out. I wanted to know what was going on, even if eavesdropping was the epitome of bad manners.

But it was better if I didn't know any more details.

I needed to simplify my life. Focus on work and volunteering and church and family. Not to mention being a foster mom. Solving mysteries was no longer my wheelhouse—especially mysteries involving the death of online dates who used fake names.

Finally, the door opened, and Drew stepped out. He smiled when our gazes connected, not the least bit shy about his interest in me.

"I'm glad we ran into each other," he said. "Unfortunate circumstances, of course. But I'd hoped our paths might cross one day."

I pushed a curl behind my ear. "Why's that?"

"Because from the first day I saw you at church, you've consumed my thoughts."

I blushed at how upfront he was. Yet it didn't seem

creepy. Instead, he struck me as chivalrous. I was a sucker for chivalry.

Drew frowned but only for a second. "That was too honest, wasn't it?"

"I can appreciate honesty."

"That's a good thing. So can I." His smile dimmed. "I do hope you'll come to Bible study at my place. It would be a great way to get to know each other a little better."

"I'll consider it."

He half nodded, half bowed. "Have a good evening, Holly."

As I watched him walk away, I noted the snug, tailored fit of his navy blue suit, the shine of his dress shoes, the way his shoulders were back and his steps were light and confident.

The real owner of that cherry-red Mustang seemed like a pretty interesting guy.

Not that that meant anything.

I turned to step into Chase's office, but instead I found him standing there, almost in the doorway. We nearly collided, but his hands reached to steady me. As soon as he touched me, fire shot through my veins, and my knees felt weak.

Why did my body still react that way to him? My physical being apparently hadn't gotten the message from my head and my heart that Chase was no longer mine. I had no right to feel this way around him.

"I'll give you a ride home," he said. "We can talk in the car."

I wondered if Chase had heard the conversation between Drew and me, but I knew he had. I didn't mention it. Instead, we walked silently outside and into his police-issued sedan. He helped me into the passenger side and then climbed in behind the wheel.

He started the car but remained in the lot, unmoving.

"I've missed you, Holly," he started, his voice raspy and sincere.

It took everything in me not to fall into his arms and pick up right where we left off. I'd wanted to spend forever with Chase. But he wasn't offering me forever. I was still having trouble coming to terms with that fact.

"I've missed you also, Chase." The emotion those words caused made my throat and eyes burn. Tears threatened to pool in my eyes.

"Are you doing okay?" His voice took on that intimate tone, the one I'd heard so many times before. Usually when I was in his arms.

I thought about his question before nodding, wondering how much to say, to share. "I've been busy. You know I bought my own place?"

"I remember you saying you were going to do that. How do you like it?"

"Honestly? It's a little lonely. I might get a roommate, but that makes it more difficult when doing foster care."

This was my first time living alone, and I wasn't loving it. But it was time for me to branch out on my own. It was past time, but when my dad had gotten cancer and then died, I'd stuck around to help out my mom. I knew I couldn't live with her forever. On the other hand, I craved people. Family. Community.

"I'm sure you'll figure it all out. How many kids have

you fostered so far?"

"Seven."

"Seven? Already?" Surprise tinged his voice.

"I've been doing respite care, so nothing that's been long term. The longest any of the children have stayed with me has been two weeks."

He shifted to face me, visibly relaxing. "Do you like it?"

I remembered all those sweet little faces who had passed through my home. Many of them had fear in their eyes—heartbreaking fear. But my time with them had been well worth the emotional struggle I felt as I tried to ease their brokenness. Those kids needed someone to be their advocate, needed someone who'd offer a shoulder to cry on.

"It's hard work," I said. "It's *heartbreaking* work, and rewarding work, and exhausting work, and it's a million other things that's hard to put into words. But I wouldn't trade the experience for anything."

"Good for you then. You're a natural when it comes to stuff like that. I know you'll make a difference in their lives."

The honesty in his words filled me with an unreasonable delight and satisfaction. "Life is short, right? We've got to make the best of it while we can."

"I can't argue with that. You've always been inspiring like that."

I crossed my ankles and turned toward him. I wanted to see his eyes so I could determine if he was telling the truth or not. "How about you, Chase? How are you?"

I really wanted to know. He had demons from his past that I knew he struggled with, including drugs, alcohol, an ex-wife, and his brother's murder. He'd also taken some flack after our last investigation for breaking the police brotherhood and turning in some unethical officers. I knew he took the brunt of their hostility since he worked around these people every day.

His face took on a more somber expression. "I've been working a lot and staying busy."

I waited for more.

He said nothing.

Finally, I nodded, accepting that I wouldn't get any more information, but disappointed that he wasn't going any deeper. I wanted more details, more emotion. But things weren't like they used to be.

"I see," I said.

The deep breath he released hinted at his inner turmoil. "I guess I should get you home so I can work on this case."

"Probably."

"One more thing I wanted to mention. If there's anything else that you remember, call me. Don't trust anyone else."

My muscles went rigid. "What do you mean?"

"It's no secret you made some enemies within the department, Holly."

I remembered that cold shoulder a few of them had given me earlier. Was that what this was about? "You really think I can't trust them? That they'd take it that far?"

"It's a possibility. And, until we know for sure, I want to be your point of contact. Understand?"

"I do." As I said the words, I glanced around. There was that feeling again. The feeling of being watched.

Was it a scorned officer, waiting for revenge? Waiting to prove a point? Or was it my overactive imagination?

I wasn't sure. And wasn't sure I wanted to find out.

CHAPTER 4

"This is my place," I told Chase ten minutes later, pointing in the distance to the little white bungalow I now called home.

Returning to this empty house had little appeal to me, especially after the events of today. But—again—I was a big girl. I could do this.

Chase pulled up to the curb, put the car in park, and leaned back. He acted as if he was in no hurry, and I wasn't sure how to interpret that.

"It looks nice." Chase ducked down so he could peer out the window. As he did, I got a whiff of his woodsy cologne. At once, memories filled me. Memories of being in Chase's arms.

As a knot formed in my throat, I pushed those thoughts away.

"It's coming along," I said, staring at my home sweet home. It was a simple craftsman-style house with a wide porch and white clapboard siding. The flowerbeds needed some work, as did the lawn. The sidewalk had some cracks in it as well. But I knew the structure and property had all the right bones to one day make it gorgeous, and it had an incredible view of downtown.

"It's going to take a while to get it in shape and make it truly my own."

He glanced up and down the street. "Not the best neighborhood, though. Have you thought about a security system?"

I was in an area known as Price Hill, which had once been beautiful. But in recent decades the allure of the neighborhood had waned as people abandoned city living to spread out to the suburbs. Crime had moved in, and it wasn't unusual to hear about this area on the nightly news—when the reporters were talking about shootings and other such things.

Frustration pinched at me at Chase's suggestion, but I held my ill feelings at bay by squeezing the life out of my purse instead. "I've considered one."

"Just a recommendation."

"Of course."

He cut the engine. "I'd feel better if I could check out the inside of the house before I left."

Alarm coursed through me. I hadn't expected that. Travis's murder was random, and my involvement was coincidental, so I shouldn't be in danger. No one was going to convince me otherwise. That feeling I had of someone watching me? It was just paranoia.

"What's that mean?" I asked.

"I mean, most likely this crime isn't in any way connected with you. But, until we have more answers, I'd feel better if we took some precautions, just to be on the safe side."

Unease shifted inside me. "Okay. If that's what you think is best."

He climbed out and, before I could follow his lead, Chase was at my door, helping me out. He walked beside me in awkward silence across the lumpy yard.

When it got warmer outside, I really needed to fix the lawn. But I had other things to worry about first. I was still painting. I might refurbish some more furniture. But spending so much time and money on the lawn and decorating seemed so frivolous, especially when I considered there were people in this area without food to eat.

Perspective.

My hands trembled when I reached the door and tried to insert my key in the lock. My nerves were showing. Wasn't that just wonderful?

I supposed I didn't want Chase to know how much he'd hurt me. Part of me wanted him to think I had everything together and that I was unaffected by our breakup. But that was crazy and prideful, two things I didn't want in my life.

"You got it?" Chase asked, standing a little too close and leaning toward me a little too much as I fiddled with the lock.

"Of course." I gave the key one last shove. It went into the lock this time. I twisted the handle, and the door opened.

"Wait here while I check things out," Chase said.

I stood back against the wall in my living room, waiting for him to return, waiting to hear his thoughts on my new place, ready for him to leave yet wanting him to stay. In other words, I felt like a mess. Like a tidal wave had ripped through my emotions and left a disaster that was impossible to clean up.

Finally, he emerged and met me by the door. "Everything is clear."

"Good to know."

He continued to linger, glancing at my walls and furniture. "Your place looks nice."

I shrugged, like it wasn't a big deal. "I'm trying."

He shifted, his hesitation unmistakable. "I should go, I guess."

I stared at him a moment before nodding. I was instinctively drawn to him. I wanted to reach my arms around his neck and give him a kiss goodbye.

After all, he'd been my first kiss. I'd been saving it for the man I was going to marry. I'd thought that man was Chase.

"If you need me, call me," he said. "I mean it."

"I will."

He hesitated another moment before nodding and stepping away. "Good night then."

"Good night, Chase."

He stepped outside and walked to his car. As he reached it, I closed the front door and latched all the locks. Then I stood there, trying to catch my breath, closing my eyes against the memories that began to pummel me.

Breaking up with him had been the right thing, I reminded myself. It had been prudent, and now I needed to move on. No more moping about it.

I sucked in a deep breath and opened my eyes.

I just needed to go to bed. It had been a long, long day.

And the image of Travis continued to haunt me, as did the feeling that I was being watched . . . even now.

***

I couldn't sleep. I wanted to. Desperately. But my mind kept replaying the events of the evening, each time ending with the body of Travis Hooker falling onto the ground.

Finally, I gave up on my quest for slumber and pulled myself out of bed. I walked across my small bedroom and hopped on the computer. I'd set it up on a little corner desk that I'd found at a second-hand store. Some white-chalk paint and distressing on the edges had made it look brand new—in a shabby sort of way.

I'd been watching way too many episodes of *Fixer Upper* lately during my sometimes sleepless nights with my foster kids.

I typed in the name "Travis Hooker" and waited while my computer considered sharing its results with me. The reveal offered surprisingly very little information. For a man who liked to toot his own horn on the dating website, Travis certainly remained low profile online. Though he had a few pages on social media, they virtually offered me no new information.

All I saw were pictures of Travis on lavish vacations, in front of fancy cars, or holding tickets to expensive concerts. How many of those things were even real? Or had he photoshopped those pictures, just like he'd altered his real name?

This was all another sign I should stay out of this.

I stared at the screen, stuck a lemon drop in my mouth, and contemplated the wisdom of what I was considering doing next.

Operation Get Over Chase was in effect. It was better to start an operation like this while I was still sleepy and delusional instead of starting it later when I was lucid and would talk myself out of it.

Out of curiosity, I typed in "Drew Williams."

I nibbled on my lip as his results popped up at me. Mostly, his online presence revolved around Wilford Funeral Home.

The man's picture stared back at me on the welcome page. I quickly scanned his bio.

Drew Williams took over Wilford Funeral Home from his grandfather four years ago. After graduating from Walnut Hills High School, he attended the University of Cincinnati. *He knows how critical these final moments are in the lives of loved ones of those who've passed, and he strives to give the best experience possible as families and friends offer goodbyes to loved ones.*

I leaned back. That sounded awfully kind and considerate.

I stared at his picture again. The man was handsome. I wondered if he had some Latin heritage—either Italian or Spanish. I wasn't sure which. But his olive skin and nearly black hair created an alluring package.

I released a shaky breath. Okay, that was my first step. Now I needed to move on. That was sufficient cyber stalking for one night.

I clicked off that link, and my fingers lingered over the keyboard another moment. I knew I shouldn't, but I clicked on Winkable.com, the dating website. I needed to remove my profile. Now. Two days ago would have been preferable. I wasn't cut out for this type of thing.

As the site loaded up, I saw four messages waiting for me. None were from Travis, so I didn't even bother to read them. Instead, I hit Delete, followed by a couple of other steps. Then I was done, gone from the site forever and ever.

I stood and stretched, realizing there was nothing else I could do. I really needed to sleep. But maybe I'd just clean my toilet real quick first. Or reorganize my silverware drawers. I settled for finding my phone and charging it.

I grabbed the device from my dresser and several new text messages caught my eye.

My heart skipped a beat when I recognized Travis's phone number.

He'd texted me? Tonight?

I held my breath as I clicked on his messages.

I'm sorry I made you a part of this.

What in the world? Why had he sent this to me?

You've got to help us.

What was he talking about? Help him what? And who was "us"? Had Travis intended on sending this to someone else, but he'd accidentally sent it to me? That's what it sounded like.

I didn't like this. I didn't like it at all.

I didn't know who else to turn to for this—

The text ended abruptly. Acid pooled in my gut. Had

Travis's text been cut short because the killer had shown up? The time stamp showed he'd sent the message only a few minutes before Jamie and I found him. Maybe five minutes earlier. I remembered because he had been ten minutes late at that point.

My eyes wandered to one last message. From Travis also. My breath caught.

It was sent only an hour ago. After Travis was dead.

My blood went ice cold.

The killer must have grabbed Travis's phone after killing him, I realized. I scanned the text, adrenaline pumping through my blood.

I know who you are. Give me what belongs to me or I'll kill you next.

What in the world? Was that message directed at me? What could someone possibly think I had that belonged to them? That was clearly a threat.

There was one thing I knew: I needed to call Chase. Again.

Because suddenly it was raining men in my life. Unfortunately, one of them was dead, and the other apparently wanted to kill me.

CHAPTER 5

Normally, I attended my childhood church on Saturday evenings and Jamie's church on Sunday mornings. But today I'd decided to head to my Saturday evening church on Sunday morning instead. Most people thought my methods were weird and unconventional—which they were.

I didn't know how to describe my choices, other than to say that my home church fed my mind with Scripture and theology, while Jamie's church fed my soul with the congregation's heart-moving worship and their emphatic amens. Between the two of them, I felt pretty balanced and ready to face the world for the rest of the week.

The congregation at my childhood church was large, and, for today, there was something exceedingly comforting about blending in and not being noticed in the crowds. Jamie's church, on the other hand, was small and met in an old strip mall. I didn't quite feel like being that social—or noticeable—today.

I slipped in late—something I never did because lateness was the same as rudeness—and I sat in the back by myself. There was a group of older widows I normally enjoyed sitting beside. Occasionally, they complained because the music was too loud and there weren't enough hymns. Sometimes they might mention how much they missed the beautiful flower arrangements that previously adorned the stage, which was now minimalistic and dark. Every once in a while, they also said they missed the pews that had been replaced with theater seating.

But these ladies were also ripe with advice and wisdom and stories from the past that captured my imagination. They could quote Scripture by memory; they were the first to volunteer to cook meals for socials; and they had some killer cake recipes.

I'd grown up here, but all my friends from childhood and youth group had either moved or gotten married. Initially, I'd still been included in their circles, even though I'd felt like a third wheel at times. But then they'd had kids, and our get-togethers had morphed into playdates. Eventually, they'd stopped inviting me, and I couldn't even be offended. I understood that groups changed with time and circumstances. We had less in common now.

There were a few singles here, but it seemed like many of them had gravitated to other churches in the area. Churches with hip, twentysomething pastors, fog machines, and lots of social media buzz that was filled with catchy, feel-good slogans.

I figured that a few minutes before church was over I'd slip out, go to my car, and I might get through the entire morning without having to interact with anyone.

It wasn't like me. I was Ms. Upbeat, Perky, and

Optimistic. But the life changes around me recently were dragging me down.

My mom was dating someone.

My sister, Alex, was expecting her first baby.

My brother, Ralph, was married to his job and trying to change the world. Or, at least, Ohio.

My best friend, Jamie, was on a mission to find a husband.

On the other hand, a possible psychotic killer was texting me and demanding I give him something I didn't have.

I'd called Chase last night and told him about the texts. He'd told me that, unlike how things happened in movies, it would be nearly impossible to trace the location of Travis's phone. He'd given two options: he could take my phone to monitor any future texts, and I could get a new one. Or I could keep my phone and keep him apprised of any new messages.

I'd opted to keep my phone and keep him updated.

As the closing song, "Blessed Be Your Name," started, I stood and grabbed my purse. That was my cue to leave.

Just as I slipped into the aisle, my phone buzzed. I fished it from my purse and glanced at the screen. I'd gotten another text from the same number.

My breath caught as I read the words there.

R U enjoying the service?

***

I paused in the back of the auditorium and scanned

the congregation. No one stood out to me. No one at all.

But the potential killer was here somewhere. He was watching me.

A shiver wiggled down my spine.

I had to get out of here. Now.

I stepped onto the plush carpet in the foyer area, my thoughts racing, and pushed my purse higher on my shoulder as I headed straight for the exit.

I was determined not to make eye contact with anyone for fear of being stopped. I just wanted to get away from whoever was watching me.

My eyes ventured up—just once—and I sucked in a deep breath at the person I saw.

Drew Williams.

Drew Williams, who looked very nice in a suit and a tie. His hair was slicked back, but not in a sleazy style. No, in one of the more popular styles of the moment. His thick and wavy locks were neatly away from his face, reminding me a bit of Gregory Peck in *Roman Holiday.*

And he saw me also, and I knew if I hurried past I would look like I had no manners at all. But there was a killer here . . .

Calming my thoughts a second, I realized that even if he was the killer, he probably wouldn't harm me right here in the foyer. No, whoever had killed Travis was methodical and well thought out.

Right now, he was trying to let me know he was a threat.

He'd succeeded.

As Drew waved at me, I slowed my steps and approached him.

Three minutes. That would be long enough to say hello and then move on without being rude.

As I got closer, I saw a gold name badge on his pocket reading "Deacon."

"Holly." He briefly touched my elbow as a grin stretched across his face. "How are you today?"

I gripped my purse. "I'm doing okay. And you?"

"I suppose that, all things considered, I'm doing okay also."

"I'm sure you're still reeling from what you learned last night," I ventured to say. I wasn't sure if I should bring it up, but why not? There was no need of skirting around the truth.

"It was quite a shock to hear that Travis was using a different name and telling you he owned my car. Part of me still has a hard time believing it. You think you know people but . . ." He ended with a headshake.

"Some people are really good at deceiving others," I finished. Unfortunately, I knew firsthand just how true that was. I'd obviously had the wool pulled over my eyes.

"Yes, they are." Drew's gaze locked on mine, and his disposition slowly morphed from disbelieving to hopeful. "Listen, Holly, do you want to grab lunch? Nothing fancy. No pressure. Just lunch."

I tried to think of an excuse. Any excuse. But, other than the fact that a killer was here and so was Drew, I couldn't. I had no other plans except to be alone and that didn't seem like a reasonable excuse to share.

And then I thought: this could be my opportunity to get information. It wasn't the best motive for lunch, but it was one of the only things that gave me the courage to say yes. Sometimes a girl just had to take what was handed to her and sort out her motivations later. Otherwise, I'd overthink everything. Every. Single. Stinkin'. Thing.

"Sure," I finally said. "Why not?"

A grin stretched across Drew's face. "Perfect. You pick where and we can meet."

"How about Kazan?" Kazan was a new Mediterranean restaurant that had opened down the street. I'd eaten there a few times and really enjoyed it.

"Sounds great." He glanced at his thick, gold watch. "I've got duty after church. I have to help enter everyone's tithes into the system. Exciting stuff, I assure you. Meet in forty minutes?"

I nodded and wondered exactly what I'd just done. "Sounds good. I'll see you there."

***

I almost changed my mind more than once. This was a bad idea. I had no right to meet with Drew, especially when I knew deep down inside that I was still hung up on Chase.

But the man had said this was just lunch. No pressure. No strings attached. I could handle that. I wasn't promising anything other than a meal together. People ate together all the time.

Despite that, my hands were trembling as I found a corner table in the quaint restaurant and waited for Drew to arrive. I was early. Of course. Because being early was actually being on time. Etiquette 101.

I glanced around the place. Thick wooden chairs gathered at matching tables; exotic tile stretched across the floor; and vintage lights hung low over the tables and expelled only the dimmest of illumination. One wall was all brick and filled with pictures taken from halfway across the world.

The smell of olive oil, lemon, and basil hit me first, followed by a hint of paprika and grilled seafood of some sort. Music—I thought it had an *Aladdin* flare, but I was sure there was a much more cultured way of describing it—floated through the overhead. This place was a nice little treasure tucked away in the city.

As I waited for Drew to arrive, my phone rang. It was Jamie. She was the perfect Rx for me now, just what I needed to talk myself off this ledge.

"How's it going today, girlfriend?" she asked. Voices filled the background, as if a crowd surrounded her.

"I got another text," I whispered.

"What? From that same guy?"

"I can only assume. It came from Travis's number. He said he hoped I was enjoying church."

She gasped. "That means he was there."

"Exactly."

"What are you going to do?"

I glanced around. "I don't know what I can do. I told Chase. But there were probably fifteen hundred people at this service. There's no way I was going to find him in that crowd."

"I can't argue with that, but you need to be careful, girlfriend."

"I will."

She paused. "Listen, do you want to come eat at church with us? My cousin Barbara brought her world-famous chicken pot pie, and there's already a line to get some. I'll fight my way to the front to reserve some for you, if you'd like. I might have to beat my baby brothers away, but it's a task I'm willing to take on for you. My momma says you need more meat on your bones anyway. Have you lost weight lately?"

I ignored her question about my weight, and I smiled at the image of her fighting for chicken pot pie. And then I began to immediately formulate a response. I pressed my lips together, knowing exactly how my explanation would sound and really not wanting to deal with her reaction. But I had no choice.

"I'm actually meeting someone for lunch," I blurted, absently rubbing my thumb across the smooth tabletop.

"It's not Chase, is it?" Concern laced her voice, and her playfulness disappeared.

"Why would you say that?" I knew exactly why. She knew I was having trouble getting over the man. She'd seen me shed tears and withdraw from my normally perky self.

"I don't know," Jamie said. "There's something about the way you look at Chase that always makes me wonder if you'll stand by your convictions."

My spine stiffened. "Of course I will."

"Don't get me wrong. I'm not saying you're wishy-washy. I just know how hard it is when your heart says one thing and your head another."

I leaned back in the chair, Jamie's words hitting me

in the gut and dropping with a dull thud. I wanted to argue, but I couldn't. "It's true. Warring within yourself is a difficult thing. I just keep trying to feed the rational side of me and starve the emotional one."

"What else can you do except act out on some sound psychological mumbo jumbo? Don't get me wrong—there's a lot of truth in that mumbo jumbo."

"But catchphrases are great to recite and much harder to live out," I finished.

"You'll get no argument from me. Everyone might say follow your heart, but God says follow Me."

"Preach it, girl," I said.

"All day, I'm living it out, girl. So, who are you meeting?" Jamie asked.

"Drew Williams."

A second passed.

"The mighty fine man from the police station?" My friend's voice lilted upward with satisfied curiosity.

Well . . . "the mighty fine man from the police station" was one way to put it. "I ran into him at church."

She let out a feisty *hm hm.* "Now this is no mumbo jumbo. Drew Williams sounds like the perfect way to get over Chase. At least one of us is having some luck."

"We're just meeting as friends," I corrected.

"Well, you have fun with your new *friend.* We'll talk later. And I want details. Lots and lots of details."

"Sounds good, Jamie." I hit End just as Drew walked inside.

He scanned the crowd. When he spotted me, his eyes lit and a smile spread across his face, instantly putting me at ease. He strode toward me and pulled out a chair.

"Sorry to keep you waiting," he started. "Even though we have a bookkeeper at the church, we always have a deacon on duty to count the offering, just for accountability purposes."

"Sounds wise. I was just catching up with my friend for a minute."

He glanced around the hole-in-the-wall. "Looks like a hidden treasure type of place. Do you come here often?"

"Only a few times. The owner's daughter is a part of the youth program where I volunteer. She invited me once, on the house. I've tried to come back since then. There's nothing like supporting local business owners, you know."

"Makes sense to me." He picked up a menu from the center of the table. "So, what's good?"

"My favorite is the Mediterranean bowl. Quinoa, olives, chicken, feta."

"You had me at olives."

"Then you'd love that dish."

He closed his menu. "It's decided then."

He flagged the waitress over. We both ordered the same dish, along with water with lemon to drink and some hummus for an appetizer.

Drew slid the menu back into place and turned to me. "So, I hardly know where to start. Asking you to tell me about yourself seems too broad and generic. How about this instead: what do you do for a living, Holly?"

"I work for Senator Ralph Paladin. I'm a community liaison."

He tilted his head. "I see."

"In full disclosure, Ralph is also my brother."

"Nothing wrong with working for family. I'm kind of fond of that myself. In fact, I think it's kind of cool. What did you do before that?"

I had to admit that Drew had great listening skills. His fingers were laced on the table, his eyes were on me and me alone, and nothing else seemed important to him.

"I was a social worker."

"Admirable career."

"I enjoyed it. It was rewarding, but it had its challenges. People are often caught up in unhealthy cycles, and their children are the ones who ultimately pay the price. Seeing the dark side of human nature can affect a person's mental well-being after a while, so the break has been nice."

He straightened his sleeves and leaned forward a bit. "I'm probably being too forward—again."

"Is this a constant problem?"

"It doesn't happen very often. Only when I meet someone who's worth being forward with."

My cheeks heated.

He must have enjoyed that reaction because a smile tugged at his lips. "I'm curious about why you were at the police station last night. Did you know Travis?"

I shook my head, feeling a touch of self-consciousness heat my cheeks again. I knew there was no shame in online dating—a lot of people did it. But it seemed so desperate to me.

"No, I didn't," I said. "Not really. My best friend—she

was with me last night at the station—convinced me I should try this dating service with her. That's how I met Travis."

Another soft smile crinkled his eyes. "I see. But the two of you had never met in person?"

"No, we were supposed to meet last night for the first time. Unfortunately, we found him . . . you know." I shrugged, not wanting to finish the sentence as images of his dead body tumbling into the street filled my thoughts.

He softened his voice. "Dead."

I nodded, compassion welling in me. "Yes, that's correct."

"I'm sorry, Holly. That must have been difficult."

"It's not my first brush with death." I realized what I'd said and how it must have sounded and startled. "It's a long story."

"You'll have to share sometime."

It was time to change the subject. Most of those stories involved Chase, and he was not a subject I wanted to bring up. "I assume you're also used to death since you're a funeral home director."

"That's correct. I grew up working for my grandfather, who started Wilford Funeral Home. He was my mom's dad. I was fascinated with the line of work."

"It takes a special person."

"I'm not going to deny that. And I don't say that as a pat on the back. But some people just aren't cut out for this kind of job. It involves being able to compartmentalize. Otherwise, you'll carry death and loss with you every day, and that isn't healthy. But you

RANDOM ACTS OF FRAUD

also have to be compassionate and unafraid to face the hard moments in someone's life. A lot of people run from those hard times. It reminds them too much of their own mortality, about the fact that one out of every one person dies."

His words somehow captured me. What Drew said was true. Not everyone was cut out to deal with death. Just as in my job as a social worker, I'd realized that not everyone was cut out to deal with harsh family situations and people who were broken—and, in return, who broke the people around them.

I'd chosen not to live life in a bubble. It seemed like Drew had also.

"It's good work you do. My cousin Chad used to be a mortician, so I know a little bit about that career choice." I shifted as the waitress delivered our hummus and water, and I took a quick sip of my ice water. "And Travis worked for you at the funeral home?"

"I hired out the company he worked for. He was a mortuary transport technician."

"Which means . . ." I dipped a pita triangle into the creamy chickpea puree.

"He was the guy who went to the coroner's office or the nursing home or the deceased's residence, and picked up the body, bringing it to the funeral home for final preparations."

"I see."

Drew shook his head, his eyes narrowing in a contemplative expression. "He seemed like a truly nice guy. I can't imagine what may have happened for him to get himself in this trouble."

Something about the way he worded it made me curious. "You mean, for someone to do this to him?"

He flinched ever-so-slightly as if he'd been caught. "Well, of course, that's what I meant."

I wasn't letting him off the hook that easily. "Or was Travis the type to get himself in trouble?"

I expected Drew to deny it. But, to my surprise, his jaw flexed, and he stared at his drink a moment before shrugging.

"Sometimes I saw that gleam in his eyes," he said. "I'm not going to lie. I had to keep my eye on him. He was a bit of a wild card, but all my clients seemed to like him."

I leaned closer. "You have no idea what might have happened to him?"

He shook his head. "I honestly have no idea what might have happened to make someone angry enough to kill him. But I do know the police have questioned his boss, as well as a grieving widower who set his targets on Travis. Hopefully, they'll find some answers soon."

Just then, my phone buzzed with an incoming text. I knew it was rude to check my phone while having a conversation. But when I considered all that had been going on lately, I wanted to know whom the message was from.

"I know this is terribly inconsiderate, but I've got to check this really quickly," I said.

"Go right ahead. I understand."

I pulled my phone out, and the words across the screen made the blood drain from my face.

R U enjoying that hummus? I'm still

waiting for you to give back what belongs to me. I know you have it, and I'm fully prepared to take action.

CHAPTER 6

"Are you okay?" Drew asked, his forehead wrinkling as he studied me.

I barely heard him. Instead, I studied the patrons around me. None looked familiar or suspicious. Everyone went about their business, enjoying their meals like normal people did on a Sunday afternoon.

But the sender of this text clearly knew I was here. He even knew what I was eating. And he wanted something from me. I had no idea what.

"Holly?"

My gaze shot to Drew. "Sorry."

"Bad news?" He nodded toward my phone.

How much did I tell him? Too much information and he'd go running. I wouldn't even blame him. Not many people would understand just how crazy my life could be sometimes.

"It's . . . complicated."

"Your ex?"

He thought Chase had texted me? I released a long breath. "Oh, no. I, um," I paused and tapped my fingernails on the table. "Whoever killed Travis apparently stole his phone and has been sending me threats."

Drew's eyes widened. "What?"

I nodded, realizing exactly how that sounded. "It's true. I have no idea what's going on or why this person feels the need to threaten little old me. But he is."

"Threaten how?"

I remembered the texter's stark words, and fear stabbed at my heart. "He hinted that he's going to hurt me unless I give him something that I don't have." I held my breath, waiting to see Drew's reaction.

He flinched, probably considering whether or not I was a loon. I mean, stuff like this didn't happen to normal people. I was totally on the same page as him regarding that.

"You told the police?" he finally asked.

"I did. They can't trace the origin of the texts, but I'm keeping them apprised of everything that happens." I smiled apologetically, before adding with fake enthusiasm, "Welcome to my life!"

Drew shifted in his seat, as if turning over his thoughts and feeling unsettled. "What could you possibly have? You said you'd never even met Travis, right?"

"That's correct. That's what makes this all even more confusing."

"Are the police patrolling by your house?"

And here went another dramatic event in my life. "Actually, several officers in our local department don't like me very much. I, um, well . . . I exposed a crime ring some of their colleagues were a part of."

"The one that was mentioned in the paper a few months ago? Some medics and others were involved?"

I nodded. "Yeah, that one."

"How did you get involved in that?"

The deeper I went into explaining this, the more I realized that this would be our first and last meal together. "It's kind of a long story. I suppose it partly has to do with me sticking my nose where it doesn't belong. And the other part has to do with the fierce need I have to see justice in this world." I frowned. "If you want to wrap up this lunch and run away from me as fast as you can, I totally understand."

He let out a quick breath. "No. No, I don't want to do that. I'm just concerned. This isn't to be taken lightly."

"It's not. But until I know who killed Travis and why, the threat is probably going to linger."

He leaned closer. "I hope you find your answers then."

"Me too." Drew hadn't run away, nor had he tried to stop me from following my instincts.

I was liking him more and more by the minute.

***

Drew and I stepped onto the street after eating at Kazan's. He'd insisted on paying, and I hadn't objected.

"Are you sure you don't need me to check out your place for you?" Drew stepped into the shade the awning above us offered from the glaring midday sun and waited for my answer.

He scored major points for being protective while

not being too protective. It was a fine line. "I'll be okay. I promise."

"If you're sure . . . I just hate to think about this guy who's been texting you living out those threats."

"I will take every precaution necessary."

He nodded, though he seemed hesitant. "Very well then. It was fun, Holly."

"It was fun." It truly had been. We'd had a nice talk over lunch, and Drew was . . . surprising.

I learned that he'd never been married, though he had been engaged once. He was on the board for a local children's charity. He loved spending time with his family, who still lived in this area, and he'd been serving as a deacon at the church for the past three years.

We'd stayed at Kazan's for three hours, and I hoped we might see each other again sometime. Drew had been a nice distraction, but it was more than that. He was good company, and we had a lot in common.

Before I could take a step toward my car, a man rammed into me.

Not again.

Before I realized what was happening, he snatched my purse and ran.

"Hey!" Drew called.

As the man sprinted down the street, Drew raced to catch him. But Drew's slick dress shoes were no match to the man's running shoes or his head start.

My heart pounded in my ears as I watched the scene unfold.

Who was that man? He'd been covered in black from head to toe. I'd barely caught a glimpse of his face. He had a hood pulled up over his head, a black bandana, and sunglasses. And everything had happened so fast.

Please don't let Drew get hurt. Please.

Finally, Drew rounded the corner. Without my purse.

His chest heaved from exertion, and sweat dotted his forehead. "I'm sorry, Holly. I couldn't catch him."

I squeezed his arm. "It's okay. Thanks for trying."

"Are you okay?" He peered at me, as if trying to ascertain my emotional state.

Little did he know that this was small potatoes compared to much of what I'd endured in the past. "I'm fine. Minus a purse, but fine."

A uniformed officer pulled up on the street just then, climbed out, and strode toward me. "Someone in the restaurant reported a purse snatching. I happened to be patrolling just down the street."

I glanced behind me and saw faces pressed against the window. None of them had their phones raised. That I could see at the moment, at least.

I observed the officer for a split second. I didn't remember seeing him before. Did he know who I was? Did he hate me like some of those other officers did?

Chase had told me to trust only him, and I had to keep that in mind.

Thankfully, Drew began filling the officer in about what had happened.

As he did, my mind wandered through everything that had occurred. This was connected with those texts I'd received. It had to be.

Someone clearly thought I had something, and he

clearly wanted it.

I just had no idea what it might be or how long this little game would continue.

***

I was humming "I've Got You Under My Skin" when I walked into my house.

Thankfully, my car keys had been in my hands when my purse was snatched. As soon as I walked inside my house, I used my landline—yes, I still had one of those—and called Chase to tell him what had happened.

He'd already heard and didn't sound happy with me. Despite that, he informed me that my purse had been located—abandoned in an alley—and he would bring it by. They hadn't caught the guy who grabbed it, however.

I decided to change while I waited for him. Then I needed to head over to my mom's house to check on things while she was out of town, just as I'd promised.

I exchanged my fitted cotton dress for a more casual knit one, and my heels for canvas tennis shoes. As I glanced at myself in my full-length mirror, I paused, one of those skin-crawling feelings causing my hairs to rise.

I scanned my bedroom, the one I'd so carefully decorated in shades of white and pale blue. My peaceful, safe place.

Why did something feel out of place?

I studied my bed. The clean lines of my white coverlet all appeared to be in place. The lacy pillows were still upright, just as I'd left them.

My gaze traveled to my dresser. My perfume was on the mirrored tray where I'd left it. My jewelry box was closed and neat.

My desk also appeared just as I'd left it, as did the gray rug with pale-blue flecks.

Everything seemed to be in place.

But that feeling still remained. The feeling that something was wrong.

That's when I saw it. A picture that I'd tucked between my mirror and its frame had tumbled off, and now hid halfway beneath my dresser. I scooped down and picked it up.

I smiled at the image there. It was a photo of Chase and me taken at the park on a beautiful sunny day last fall. He stood behind me with his arms blanketing me. The smiles on our faces were enough to make anyone believe we were in love. Because we had been in love.

It was just that true love didn't always conquer all, despite what the songs said. How we felt about each other did nothing to change how both of us felt about the future.

I stared at the picture another moment before opening my top drawer and sliding the photo inside. I probably should have done this a long time ago, but I'd been delaying it. I'd been in denial maybe, hoping desperately that Chase would change his mind.

It was time to let that go.

I supposed the fallen picture had been what caused my skin to crawl. There was nothing to be concerned about. The creepy-crawly feeling was just a culmination of everything that had happened over this weekend. My fears were messing with me.

I reached into my closet to find a lightweight coat, like my jean jacket. I wanted something to cover my arms, just in case the wind was chilly, as it was prone to be on occasion in April. But my jacket wasn't where I'd hung it.

I stepped back, trying to retrace my steps. I'd definitely hung it up here after my date with disaster last night.

I shoved a few items of clothing out of the way and finally spotted the denim in a heap on the floor. It must have fallen off its hanger.

As I slipped the coat over my arms, something tumbled out of the pocket and onto the well-used wood floors of my bedroom.

I retrieved the object and stared at it for a moment. A key dangled from an empty chain—well, empty except for a broken metal square on the end. There were no words or numbers on the key, no hints as to what it might belong to.

Where in the world had this come from?

The scene from last night replayed in my head. The man who'd run into me on the sidewalk.

Had he somehow slipped this into my pocket?

I didn't have any other ideas. Could this be what the man who was texting me wanted? A key? Was that what this was all about?

Dread pooled in my stomach.

Thankfully, at that moment, my doorbell rang. Chase. I had to give this to him.

CHAPTER 7

Chase wasn't officially working today, so it wasn't a surprise when he showed up wearing jeans with a henley instead of his normal khakis and a button-up shirt. My heart stuttered a beat when I saw him.

Traitor. My heart should know better. Yet every time I saw him it reacted like this, like a dog who couldn't stop wagging its tail when he saw the owner who'd abandoned him.

"Holly." He stood at my front door with his hands on his hips, like he was ready to take charge of the situation. First, he handed me my purse. "I don't know if anything is missing or not. Maybe you can tell us."

I took it from him before extending my hand behind me. "Come on in."

He strode inside the house, and, as always, his frame—his being—seemed to fill the space in its entirety. Kind of like he'd filled my heart at one time.

Quickly, I glanced through my purse. Everything appeared to be here, including my wallet and cell phone. That was good news, at least.

"I'm glad you're here. I need to show you something. Can I get you some coffee first?" My throat felt achy as I said the words, but I desperately wanted some normalcy now.

Today had been crazy. This whole weekend had been crazy, for that matter. And it had all started with online dating. I should have known better.

He paused ever so slightly and released a small breath, looking as tense as I felt. When would this ever get easier?

Breakup etiquette rule number five: create a new support system.

And yet Chase was the only cop I could trust enough to call.

This was a problem.

"Actually, coffee sounds great," he finally said.

I wondered what he'd been doing to make him so tired. Working? Exercising? Maybe he was dating someone else—a thought that shouldn't bother me but did.

"Follow me," I said.

We went into the kitchen, and I began scooping some grounds into the coffeemaker.

"How are you doing today?" I asked, trying to make some polite small talk. I turned the pot on and listened as it gurgled, and the bitter aroma of coffee began floating through the air.

"I guess I can't complain. How about you?" He settled against the counter across from me and folded his arms. All of this felt too normal, too ordinary for my tastes.

"Still a little shaken from last night. I don't suppose you'd tell me if you had any updates." I rubbed my hands together and waited. He had to be used to me asking these kinds of questions. I did it all the time. Or I *had* done it all the time in the past.

"It's an ongoing investigation. I can tell you that we're still gathering information on Travis Hooker. I was up most of the night working on the case."

Relief filled me. That was why he was tired. Not that I cared.

"I understand." The pot sputtered, giving me a good excuse to turn around and grab a coffee mug. I poured Chase a cup, quickly choosing a mug that showed a vintage New York City skyline. At once, I wanted to take it back, and I hoped he didn't get the wrong idea.

Chase and I had talked about going to New York together one day. I'd assumed that day would be after we were married. I had no idea what Chase was thinking as he took the coffee from me. Did he think I was hinting at something? Badgering him? Trying to guilt trip him?

But he didn't seem to react, so I was probably reading too much into it.

"Do you know how Travis died?" I finally asked. "Can you tell me that?"

"We believe he may have been poisoned."

A chill washed through me. Poisoning would take some premeditation. And premeditation would mean that the killer hadn't done this on accident or even in the heat of the moment. It meant that someone had planned it.

"We do have one lead," he said. "I know I'm sharing more than I should, but I hope it will prevent you from pursuing anything on your own."

"Why, I would never," I said in my best Scarlet O'Hara accent.

Chase chuckled sardonically. "Yeah, we won't go there. But we're looking at Travis's boss."

I sucked in a breath. "Drew Williams?"

"No. Drew hired out the company that Travis worked for."

That was right. My mind had jumped to worst-case scenarios. Of course.

"Travis's boss was giving him a hard time," Chase continued. "Apparently, several clients had complained about Travis also."

"Complained how?" I asked.

"I guess he wasn't using the best bedside manner when he went to pick up the deceased from people's homes."

Funny that Drew hadn't mentioned that. Did he know? "I'm sorry to hear that. That's a very stressful time in people's lives, one that requires extra sensitivity."

"It is. The boss had confronted Travis several times. The company started losing some business because of bad word of mouth."

I leaned back, letting that information sink in. "So, the boss—what's his name again?"

Chase scowled and reluctantly said, "Ronald."

"Ronald Dillow, correct? The owner of Dillow Mortuary Transportation?"

"How'd you know that?"

I shrugged innocently. "I have my ways. Anyway,

you think Ronald killed him? That's extreme."

"There's more. His boss has a history of flying off the handle. He was arrested and did some jail time for assault. The GPS on his phone also shows he was downtown that evening."

I shivered. "I see. But a man like that . . . with those demons and that temperament . . . he doesn't seem like someone who'd poison someone. Someone that angry would strangle someone first or maybe shoot him."

Chase twisted his head, as if my observation surprised him. "That's true. But human nature can be unpredictable sometimes. He's our best lead."

"Well, I hope it all pans out. Maybe Travis realized that his boss was really angry. Maybe that's why he sent me those messages before we were supposed to meet."

"You think Ronald Dillow was up to something illegal?" Chase asked.

"I assume you've looked into it. I mean, that would make the most sense, right? Maybe Travis had discovered Ronald was doing something illegal—drugs, maybe?—and he was going to turn him in. Ronald found out and killed him before he could."

"Interesting theory."

I paused. "You have no idea what Travis might have been poisoned with?"

"I don't. We're still waiting for the tox screen to come back." He took a sip of his coffee before lowering the drink and locking his gaze on mine. "So, you found something?"

"Yes. That's right." I snapped out of my stupor. That was the whole reason Chase was here. I couldn't forget that. And here I'd been thinking he'd just come by to torture me by dangling memories of our relationship in front of me. "Let me grab it."

I hurried back to my bedroom and snatched the key from my dresser. I halfway hated to give it up. This was some kind of clue to something. I just had no idea what. At the moment, it was my *only* clue.

"You put it in a bag?" Chase's eyebrows shot up.

"I didn't want to mess up any fingerprints."

"I taught you well." He flashed a smile.

"That you did." Usually through the school of hard knocks, one where I'd interfered and he'd had to correct me.

He held up the bag and examined the key through the plastic. "You really think that man put this in your pocket last night? The guy who ran into you?"

"It's the only thing I can figure." I'd replayed the event a million times. Maybe that *had* been a flash of recognition I'd seen in the man's gaze. Yet he wasn't familiar to me. There was so much I didn't understand.

"I'll see if we can figure out who this belongs to. It's a long shot."

I hoped he might offer more, but he remained silent. I needed to accept that I wouldn't get any more information from him and be thankful that he'd shared anything. "Well, I hope you're able to figure out what's going on."

He stared at me a moment, that probing look returning. "Would you like to go get something to eat, Holly?"

I wasn't sure I could handle that. I was going to

tumble back into a pit of confusion and overwhelming emotions that warred with my logic. Space was the best thing I could give myself now. Besides, breakup etiquette dictated that I should maintain my distance from Chase for a while.

"I can't, Chase. I've got to run by my mom's house."

He stood straight and put the coffee mug onto the counter. "I understand. Maybe another time."

"Yeah, maybe another time." But not if I was smart.

I walked him to the door, hating the angst gripping me. Only moments earlier I'd been reveling at how happy I'd felt after lunch with Drew. Things could change on a dime sometimes, couldn't they? Circumstances. Emotions. Plans for the future.

It could be worse, I supposed.

I could be Travis Hooker.

***

I was just locking up my mom's place when I felt someone on the porch behind me.

The image of Travis's lifeless body slammed into my mind. Instinctively, I reached into my purse and grabbed my pepper spray. I twirled around, ready to act, to defend myself.

A woman stood on my steps. Her eyes zeroed in on my pepper spray, and she gasped, throwing her hands in the air. Her purse fell from beneath her arm, and its contents scattered all over the sidewalk.

"I'm sorry," she rushed. "I wasn't trying to sneak up on you."

I stared at the woman a moment. She looked . . . I blinked. She looked surprisingly like me with her auburn hair, a slim build, blue eyes.

She didn't dress anything like me, however. No, she wore skin-tight skinny jeans with heels and a sweater that hugged her curves. She also had a small nose ring and a curly-cue from a tattoo peeked out from beneath her sleeve.

"Who are you?" I asked, not letting down my guard yet.

I'd learned to be cautious. Maybe paranoid. I wasn't sure. But too many scary situations had stared me in the face recently. *Victim no more.*

"I'm looking for Holly Paladin."

I kept the spray raised. "I'm Holly."

She rubbed her hands on her jeans and drew in a long, deep breath. "I figured that. We look alike. Eerily so."

"I noticed," I said. "Have we met before?"

"No, we haven't. But I think we might . . . we might be . . . cousins."

CHAPTER 8

I froze, unsure what to say. I'd met all my cousins before, and this woman wasn't one of them. "Why would you think that?"

She hooked a hair behind her ear. "I hate to go into everything right here. I know I'm putting you on the spot. But long story short is that I believe my mom and your father were siblings."

The color drained from my face, and I lowered the pepper spray as the truth nudged closer to me. "What?"

She nodded. "Can we chat?"

Against my better instincts, I pointed to the porch. "Why don't you have a seat? It sounds like we do have some things to discuss."

I wasn't going to let her inside. No, I wasn't quite that trusting. But, today was gorgeous, especially right now as the sun began sinking in the sky. Besides, my mom's yard was practically from *Better Homes and Gardens*, so the porch would be just fine. Especially since the azaleas were blooming.

I knew exactly the truth this woman was hinting at, and it seemed like it couldn't be true. But our resemblance was uncanny. I wanted to hear what she

RANDOM ACTS OF FRAUD

had to say, even if it turned my world upside down.

"Have a seat." I nodded toward some wicker chairs on the porch of the Tudor style home. "Can I fix you something to drink?"

She squatted and picked up several things that had fallen from her purse. "Do you have lemonade?"

I should help her gather her things. But first I needed to clear my head. It was my top priority at the moment.

"Lemonade?" I repeated. "Absolutely. One minute."

What was the etiquette for this? My *Book of Manners* didn't exactly cover what to do if someone claiming to be your cousin showed up, and I had no idea how to handle this situation.

Thankfully, I was able to escape inside and collect my thoughts, even if just for a moment.

***

My family had only recently discovered that my father was adopted. His family was wonderful, but his parents were both dead now—they'd been older, and he had no siblings.

Part of me wanted to leave the past in the past. What good would it do me now to learn the details of my father's birth family? I supposed that somewhere down the line there could be medical reasons as to why this could be important. It would also give me hints about my heritage and would help me learn my family's history.

With the lemonade mixed, I poured the drinks. I also

put a few sugar cookies on a tray and carried everything outside. My possible cousin had taken a seat in a navy blue wicker chair, just as I'd suggested. She lounged there, her legs crossed, and stared out at the street in front of her, as if in deep thought.

She snapped out of it when she sensed me beside her.

"I didn't catch your name," I started as I set the tray down on the table between us.

"I'm sorry." She shook her head and sat more upright. "My name is Blake. Blake Hallowell."

"Nice to meet you." I rubbed my hands together.

She glanced behind her. "Nice place you have here."

"It was a dump when my mom and dad bought it, but they restored it," I said. "I think it's pretty great as well."

Blake gripped her sweaty glass and shifted to face me. "You grew up here?"

"I did. I just got my own house a few months ago. It's not too far from here."

"But far enough, right?"

"I suppose. But I do miss this place. It's home, and it always will be. How about you? Where do you live?"

"I just moved here from Hillsboro. I'm starting the doctorate program at UC in the fall. Business administration. Exciting, huh? I came early to take a couple of summer courses. They just started last week."

"What do you want to do with your degree?"

"I know this sounds sad, but I'm not really sure. Maybe that's why I went back to school—to buy myself more time." She smiled sheepishly.

"At least you can be honest about it."

She raised her eyebrows, a hint of disappointment wrinkling her forehead. "It's one thing I've got going for me."

Silence stretched a moment as we both sipped our drinks, and Blake grabbed a cookie. I was avoiding the most important questions, but all other small talk escaped me for a moment, leaving me no choice but to jump in.

"So . . ." I started, then rubbed my lips together.

"I know this is surprising." She glanced at her lemonade. "But my grandmother died in November. Right before she passed, she confessed that she'd had a baby when she was eighteen, but her parents had pressured her to give the child up for adoption. With no real means to support herself, she felt like she had no choice. They were different times back then. Teenage pregnancy . . . well, it was totally frowned upon, to say the least."

I held my breath. I knew where this was going. I thought I did, at least. And it all seemed surreal.

"Three years later, she met my grandfather, and they got married. They had three other children. But my grandmother never forgot about her firstborn. The adoption was closed, and she assumed it was best that she keep it that way."

"Okay." I waited, hardly able to breathe as I anticipated what she'd say next.

"Needless to say, that made me curious. So I started trying to find her baby, my uncle. It took a lot of digging, but I finally found a name. Herbert Paladin."

Though I'd been expecting her announcement, my breath caught. My dad.

"Herbert was my father." My voice cracked. "He passed away almost three years ago."

She nodded, a mix of apology and concern on her face. "I discovered that also. I wasn't sure if you would welcome me or not, but I figured I didn't have anything to lose. I wanted to meet my uncle's family. None of my own family knows I'm doing this. I didn't want to get their hopes up."

I wasn't quite ready to make the leap from *could be* cousins to *definitely were* cousins. I needed more information first.

"You really think we're related?" I asked.

"I'm nearly certain."

I leaned back, still gripping my drink like a lifeline. "I don't even know what to say. It would explain why we look so much alike, I suppose."

"Did you know your father was adopted?" she asked quietly.

"My mom and I discovered that information only a few months ago. We had no idea before that. I'm not sure if my father even knew."

"I don't think people talked about it as much back then."

"I think you're right." I put my drink down before I spilled it on myself. There were questions that needed to be asked. What were they? "I'm sorry. I'm still processing this. It's . . . a lot."

"I'm sure it must be." Blake shifted, also putting her drink down. "Look, I'm not looking for anything. I just thought it would be fun to connect with you all. I think a person's history is important."

I agreed and released my breath, some of my tension easing. "Tell me more about your family."

"We're pretty simple. We live in the country. My dad is a chicken farmer. It's beautiful up where we live. If you like the country, that is. The roosters really do wake us up in the morning, and we've been known to cow tip on occasion."

"It sounds nice. Simple. Unless you're a cow."

She offered a brief smile. "I have eight other cousins. The oldest is thirty-five. The youngest is nine. We have family dinners every weekend."

"That sounds amazing." The rest of my cousins lived out of the area, so I only saw them a few times a year. My family gatherings were mostly just us—my mom, my brother, my sister, her husband, and me.

"It was a great childhood." She glanced at her hands. "Did my uncle have a good life?"

"He did." My voice caught. I still missed my father so much. Cancer had taken him from us too early. "He was the best dad ever."

"I'm glad. And you have a brother and sister?"

"That's right. My sister, Alex, is a district attorney. Ralph is a state senator. I come from a long line of overachievers. But my dad wasn't like that. He preferred to take life in stride and do what he enjoyed."

"I can respect that."

"How'd you find out that your uncle might be my father? The adoption was closed, correct?" Finding biological children and birth mothers after a closed adoption was difficult, to say the least.

"Yes, but I found this online website for closed adoptions where people can post ads. They usually include a birthdate, sex, and basic area of the country. People match that data with what they know. I found one that fit what my grandmother told me about the child she'd given up."

"Who left that ad?" My mom? Would she have done that? It seemed out of character for her.

Blake shrugged. "I'm not sure. There wasn't a profile with it, only the user name: Inquiring in Cincinnati. In fact, I emailed the person who posted a few times but never heard anything. I finally started searching through online information for males born on May 6, 1960, who lived in Cincinnati. I came across an article on Herbert Paladin—something about a large birthday party he'd had on his fiftieth."

I smiled and remembered that article. My mom was known for her parties, so she'd planned a surprise one in honor of my father. Instead of guests bringing gifts, they brought donations for a local animal shelter. A reporter had come and done a story on the whole shindig.

"The dates matched up?" I concluded. "His birthday with what your grandmother told you?"

"That's right. I still wasn't sure that he was the right person. I figured since I was already here in Cincinnati, I might as well see what else I could find out."

"It looks like you did an amazing job piecing everything together." Which could be more evidence that we were possibly related. It seemed like something

I would do.

More silence stretched. This was all very compelling, but it still didn't prove anything. How did you prove something like this?

"So, what do we do now?" I asked.

Blake gently touched her nose ring, twirling it like it was uncomfortable. "I'm not sure. I suppose there might be tests to confirm this."

"DNA testing?" I said. "We need something more than a birthday, right?"

"Possibly."

"When my mom gets back, I'll run this past her. How's that sound? I don't want to make such a huge decision for my family without their input."

"I understand. Maybe we can connect more then?"

"Yes, that sounds good."

She let out a long breath and stared back at the street where a steady stream of traffic passed. It wasn't just traffic. It was obnoxious traffic that included loud music, people hollering out windows, and lots of honking horns. *Welcome to my neighborhood.*

"You know, you're the first person I've met since I've been here who seems like a friend. Granted, I've only been here for less than a month now, and my core grad classes haven't started yet. Either way, it's been a pretty lonely stay here. I'm glad we met because now it seems like coming here may have been a good idea."

"I'm glad. Slightly overwhelmed, but glad."

"It's understandable." She handed something to me. "Here's my contact information. I'd love to get to know you better. But I'm going to leave the ball in your court."

I took the paper where she'd scribbled the information. "I'll give you my number also. Everyone needs to have someone they can depend on when they move to a new place. If you need anything, I have some pretty fantastic connections."

She smiled. "I hope we'll be able to see each other again sometime."

I nodded. "Me too."

CHAPTER 9

That evening, Jamie came over.

I needed someone to discuss all of this with, and she'd been more than willing to help. It didn't hurt that I'd made her favorite cookies—gluten free, of course. We sat on my back deck, watching the sunset smear hues of pink behind the city skyline, and listening to the city life around us: distant sirens, traffic, neighbors talking too loudly.

We rehashed what I knew, beginning with the text-based threats, moving to the key I'd found, and ending with my mysterious cousin showing up.

"I know I should stay out of this," I muttered.

"But you just can't help yourself, can you?"

She knew me all too well. "What if I only kind of get involved? Not like jumping in with both feet, but maybe I could just poke around a bit?"

"If this guy keeps threatening you, you may not have any choice."

"So I should be proactive," I concluded.

"When you put it that way . . ."

"Okay, now that that is decided, this is what I know." I pulled my legs beneath me as I made myself comfortable on the wicker chair and its cheerful yellow cushion. "Travis Hooker liked to live large, using a different name, a different car, and a made-up career. I highly doubt he could even afford half of the things he talked to me about."

"That sounds about typical."

"He probably liked dating sites because they allowed him to be someone he wasn't," I continued, pretending like I was much better at this psychological profiling thing than I actually was. "He could impress people, and they were none the wiser about it."

"Welcome to dating in the twenty-first century." Jamie popped another cookie into her mouth and narrowed her eyes like she was bitter about having to suffer through modern dating.

"Chase told me Travis might have been poisoned. He also told me they found a puncture mark on Travis, which leads me to believe that he was poisoned through some kind of injection. We have to consider who would have access to that kind of poison."

"They don't know what it was yet?"

"If they know, Chase hasn't told me."

Jamie wiped the crumbs from her lap. "That makes me think of someone with a medical background."

"It very well could be, although drug users use syringes, so maybe not."

"True that."

"I've also gotten those strange texts, texts that make it sound like Travis was going to turn someone in. There's obviously some kind of information or evidence out there that terrifies someone—terrifies someone enough that they're willing to kill to keep it quiet."

"So, it must be something pretty serious."

"I would think so," I said. "This isn't a case of you stole my girlfriend or ruined my car or got the promotion I wanted. There's more to it."

"I agree."

"Then, there's also the man who ran into me on Saturday. He must have left that key, so he was somehow involved in this whole fiasco. Maybe when he told me to be careful he was talking about this very scenario."

Jamie pushed the plate of cookies away. Yes, even too much gluten-free food could be bad for you. "Why did he leave the key with you, though?"

I replayed the scene in my head. "I thought I saw a moment of recognition on the man's face. What if he was friends with Travis? What if he was headed toward Travis with some kind of information, he ran into me, and he recognized me from the dating site? Maybe Travis showed him my picture."

"That's plausible."

"So, this guy left that key with me for some reason. He wanted me to have it, though I can't imagine why. I have no idea what ended up happening to him. Maybe he disappeared."

"Could have. Hard to say since we don't know who he is."

"I've also felt like I'm being watched. Maybe the killer is keeping an eye on me. Maybe he wanted that key, and he snatched my purse, hoping it was inside."

"He thought Chinstrap Beard guy had given it to you,

and you were just trotting around with it in your purse? And how would he know you had it?"

I shrugged. "Beats me. I have no idea. Maybe he tortured Chinstrap Beard guy until he confessed."

Jamie's eyebrows shot toward the sky. "This is sounding a lot like a scene from the Bourne trilogy. Go on."

"I know that Travis had been having problems with his boss, Ronald Dillow, and that people had complained because Travis wasn't acting in a reassuring manner to the families of the deceased."

"Maybe something happened to stress him out. Maybe he discovered something his boss was doing and it messed with his head. That could explain his texts. Maybe he collected evidence against the Ronald guy."

"That could be it. There was one other man mentioned, someone whose wife had died when a drunk driver hit her a few months ago. He had a lot of anger built up toward Travis."

"Enough anger to kill him?"

"Maybe." I shrugged.

"Why would this guy be mad at Travis, though?"

"I have no idea." I grabbed my laptop—I'd brought it out with me, just in case an occasion like this arose—and did a quick search. Ronald Dillow's picture popped up, and I showed it to Jamie. "He doesn't look anything like the man who tried to snatch my purse. He's too heavy and out of shape."

The man was balding, and everything about him struck me as round—his head, his body, his eyes. But his smile seemed sincere enough.

She tossed her head back and forth in thought. "He could have hired someone."

"I suppose. But I still have trouble believing it's him. Chase said he has anger problems. Someone who's angry doesn't meticulously plan to poison someone."

"Good point."

I tapped something else into the computer, deciding to go in a different direction. "Okay, I just typed 'Cincinnati,' 'woman killed,' 'drunk driver,' and 'February.'"

"Did anything pop up?" Jamie snatched one more cookie.

I nibbled on my bottom lip. "Only one that fits all that criteria. Dan Gilbert. He's a doctor."

I stared at his picture. He appeared, from the photo, to be tall and well built. Could he be the man who'd tried to snatch my purse?

"Does he look familiar?" Jamie asked.

"Without seeing him in real life, it's hard to know." As my words hit my ears, an idea formed.

My eyes connected with Jamie's.

"Are you thinking what I'm thinking?" she asked.

I shrugged, trying to look more casual than I felt. "Maybe we should go check this guy out."

"Okay, okay" She raised a hand. "That's my first impulse too, but let's think this through: what good would it do to track down Dan Gilbert?"

"I want to see his face," I said. "See if I recognize him or the way he walks."

"I don't know about that. Are we just asking for trouble?"

That was a great question. "Not if we're smart about how we handle this. We keep our distance. We observe. And that's it. Besides, I just can't keep sitting here being a victim. I need answers. This guy is threatening to kill me, Jamie. Until I know who he is, I'm powerless to stop him—or to let the police stop him, I should say."

She stood and saluted. "I can respect that. Let's go. Because ain't nobody killing my best friend."

***

"This is where he lives?" Jamie peered out the window of my Mustang and munched on another cookie. "He could stay in that house for a week and never need to come out."

Dr. Dan Gilbert did live in a very large home in a very affluent area of town. His house was three stories and brick. He had a large, manicured lawn, and a gate surrounded the property. Houses just like his—only different—lined the street.

We sat on the dark street, one with nice curvature, no potholes, and smooth sidewalks. In other words, it was nothing like my neighborhood.

We hadn't parked under a streetlight but a little farther down instead. I made myself comfortable, taking my seat belt off and shifting my legs beneath me.

And, now that I was here, I had no idea why I was here. What did I want to prove by being here? Did I think I'd see Dan Gilbert lurking around with a gun in his hand?

Just then, someone banged on my window.

I nearly jumped out of my skin as I turned toward the sound.

Dan Gilbert stood there with a gun in his hand, leering at me.

"You've got to be kidding me," I muttered.

Before I realized what was happening, he jerked the door open and grabbed me by the shirt collar. In a split second, he pulled me from the driver's seat and threw me against the car.

I didn't have time to breathe. To scream. To think.

"What are you doing here?" he sneered.

The man was solid. And scary.

He had dark hair that was buzzed nearly to the scalp. A square face. Broad shoulders. A scar at his temple. He was like an angry Rambo doctor man.

Scarier still, the veins at his neck bulged and his eyes were bloodshot.

I tried to suck air into my lungs, but my body felt too jarred. "I'm . . ."

"You're what?" He rammed me into the car again.

"I'm . . . investigating Travis Hooker."

He loosened his grip on me but only slightly. "Tell me more before I crush your windpipe."

This guy sounded serious, and I had no doubt he knew exactly how to squeeze my neck until breathing was a distant memory.

"Ever since he died, someone has been threatening me," I explained, hoping to get through to him before he killed me. "I'm trying to figure out what kind of trouble Travis got into before he died. Maybe then I can figure out how to get this person off my back."

His nostrils flared. "You're his friend?"

"No, I'm not his friend. But someone thinks I am. Or something." I was making myself sound suspicious. Not good. Not good at all.

"Tell me more," he growled. "Now."

"Where's your bedside manner, Doctor?" Jamie climbed from the car and raised her own gun. "Take your hands off of her."

Thankfully she had a conceal carry permit, and she wasn't afraid to use it.

"Put the gun down or I'll shoot your friend," Dan barked.

"Then I'll shoot you," Jamie said.

"Good. Put me out of my misery. I don't have any reason to live."

My heart rammed into my rib cage even harder than before. This man was desperate, with nothing to lose. That was never a good sign.

"I'm sure you have a lot of reasons to live," I told him softly.

"My wife is dead. I'm in danger of losing my medical license. I've got nothing. Nothing!"

"Killing me won't help," I said.

"It won't matter."

"You can restore what's been lost. It's never too late." I had to somehow get through to him before he did something he'd regret, and before he took away the opportunity for me to regret something I'd done.

"You're a Pollyanna if I've ever heard one." He scowled again.

"Please, Dr. Gilbert," I whispered. "I'm not ready to

die. Not yet. I've got to figure out what Travis Hooker was up to first."

He stared at me a moment.

I really wished he'd put that gun down. And let me go.

As if he'd heard my prayers, he released me. I scrambled away, desperate to put distance between us. I joined Jamie on the opposite side of the car. I could hardly hear anything over the sound of my heart pounding in my ears.

"Travis Hooker ruined my wife!" he barked.

"Was he the one driving the car that hit her?" Jamie asked.

"No."

"Then how did he ruin her?" I asked, still painfully aware of the gun he held and how precarious this situation was.

"We brought her home after her accident and thought she was going to be okay. It was going to be a long process. A long recovery. But then she had an aneurism." His facial muscles tightened. "Travis was one of the guys who came to get her body. He asked for privacy while he loaded her on the gurney. But I couldn't stand being away from her. I opened the door, and I found him going through her lingerie drawer."

Nausea pooled in my stomach. That was horrible. Disgusting. Distasteful. But was it really a good reason for all this anger?

It didn't matter. He thought it was a good enough reason, and that was all that mattered right now.

"I'm sorry, Dr. Gilbert. But don't make more people

suffer. Please." My voice took on a pleading tone.

He showed no response.

"You didn't kill Travis, did you?" I asked. He was already angry, and I hoped my question didn't put him over the edge. However, he already seemed like he was way over that edge and freefalling into an abyss of uncontrollable emotions.

"Kill him? No, I wanted to send him to prison so he'd suffer."

Okay, that was a good start. "Where were you last night?"

"I was at Speedy's Bar all night. Ask anyone there."

"You're not a killer, Dr. Gilbert. You help heal people." I prayed my words would calm him down and bring him to his senses. "I know you are. I read those articles that quoted people whose lives you saved. Whose lives you changed and impacted for the better. Don't throw all that away."

I actually hadn't read that, but I hoped it was true.

He stared at me a moment—a cold, hard stare. I had no idea what he would do. I feared he'd raise his gun and do something drastic.

Instead, he stepped back.

"Get out of here," he grumbled. "But if I see you two again, I won't hesitate to use excessive force next time."

CHAPTER 10

Jamie and I stared at each other once we were far away from Dan Gilbert's house. I didn't know about Jamie, but my heart was pounding out of control.

Dan Gilbert had a murderous look in his eyes, and I'd believed every word he'd said.

"He would have access to syringes," Jamie said once we sat outside my house. "He's a doctor."

"That's true." I nodded stiffly, still feeling dazed.

"He has anger management problems."

"Also true," I said.

"He hated Travis."

"That he did." I glanced at Jamie. "Is he our guy? Did he kill Travis and now he wants some information that Travis collected on him? Maybe Travis wanted revenge so he somehow got his hands on some less-than-flattering information concerning the doctor. There are all sorts of things Dr. Gilbert could be mixed up in. Illegal prescriptions. Medical malpractice. Sexual harassment in the work place."

"There's only one reason why I'd say he wasn't behind the crime." Jamie tapped her chin. "He didn't seem to recognize you."

I thought about her words. They were true. He didn't seem to recognize me at all. "If he was the bad guy, he would have known who I was."

"We could check his alibi, at least."

"I agree."

I leaned back in the seat, wondering about the wisdom of remaining in this car after so many things had happened. Wouldn't the inside of my house be safer?

"So where does this leave us?" I asked.

"Back to square one, I suppose. What about Travis's boss—that Ronald guy?"

"I can see what I can find out about him. You're right—he could have hired people to do his dirty work."

"He's the only other person I can think of who might have a motive."

I stared at the dark street in front of me, my hands still trembling from my encounter with Dan the Unhinged. "I just think there's something bigger going on here, Jamie. I don't know what. I don't know how to find out what. I don't know if I should even attempt to find out what. But something's not right with this whole scenario. We've got to figure out what before someone else dies."

"There's only one thing I can think of to do next," Jamie said.

"What's that?"

"Go eat Indian food."

I blinked at her, trying to follow her line of thought. "Why in the world would we do that? Are you having a late-night craving or something?"

"For Indian food? No way. But you said the man who ran into you on Saturday smelled like curry. We have very few leads here. We've got to use whatever we've got. Maybe someone in the restaurant remembers him and could give us a clue as to who he is."

My friend was brilliant. I should have thought of this myself—and I should have thought of it earlier. But I hadn't, so there was no time like the present to find answers.

"I like how you think," I said. "Let's go."

***

No sooner had Jamie and I been seated at Bombay Joe's and ordered some carrot halwa, did a familiar figure stride into the restaurant.

Chase.

And his laser eyes, which seemed to have a tracking device targeted to find me, went right to our table.

His face darkened, and he bypassed the hostess and charged right toward me.

He knew me well enough to know why I was here; this wasn't a coincidence. But what I wondered was why he was here. Certainly, this had been one of the first places he'd come. The fact that he'd returned three days after the crime must mean this place was significant.

"Jamie." He nodded tersely at my friend before nodding even more tersely at me. "Holly. Fancy running into the two of you here."

I rolled my shoulders back. "What a small world."

"Not really."

Before I could object, he slid in beside me. As soon as our shoulders brushed, my entire body felt rigid. Or was it alive? The lines were so blurry sometimes.

"Do you two want to tell me what you're doing here? And don't tell me you came for the mango ice cream."

"It was for the carrot halwa, actually." I raised my chin higher.

"The what?"

"It's this carrot pudding. It has—" I stopped myself. "Never mind."

Even I knew I wouldn't sound convincing if I tried to tell him how good it was. Carrot pudding wasn't exactly my dessert of choice. Ever. Chase would know me well enough to know that.

"Uh-huh," Chase muttered.

I laced my fingers together. "And what brings you here?"

He stared at me, a half flash of amusement, half flash of frustration twinkling in his eyes. "I think you know why I'm here."

"You're stalking me?"

He let his head fall toward his shoulder. "Really?"

"You had a hankering for Indian food?"

"Never."

"Then I'm all out of guesses."

He sighed and leaned back. "I know I don't need to tell you this, but you shouldn't get involved in this investigation."

"Involved would be a strong word," I argued. "I'm

having carrot pudding."

The waitress delivered our dish right then, and both Jamie and I lost our appetite when we saw it. We'd chosen the carrot dessert because Jamie thought she could eat it since it was gluten free. It was apparently free from any appeal also—unless you really liked carrots.

"By all means, go ahead and enjoy it." Chase nodded at the dish.

As a surge of pride rose in me, I lifted the spoon, determined to save face. I scooped up a decent sized spoonful and daintily placed it in my mouth, careful to appear like I was eating a delicacy.

As the texture hit my taste buds, I fought the urge to gag.

I'd never really liked carrots. Or pudding. I was more of a cookie and pie gal.

Despite that, I forced myself to swallow. "Delicious. Do you want to try some?"

"I'll pass." Chase stared at me, making no attempt to hide the fact that he was onto me.

Jamie cleared her throat. I'd nearly forgotten she was there, and she'd noticed. She sounded slightly offended as she asked, "Did you check out Dr. Gilbert's alibi?"

"Numerous witnesses verified he was at the bar almost all night."

"Any updates on Ronald Dillow?" I asked.

Chase finally broke his gaze and released a subtle breath. "None that I can share."

I guessed when we stopped dating I lost my

privileges of getting little snippets on his cases. Of course, he'd never shared anything that he was professionally banned from saying. But occasionally he would reveal things he'd learned that were within reason.

"Is there anything you can share?" Jamie continued.

His voice was all business when he responded, "No."

That answered the question for me as to whether or not he'd be forthcoming. He was playing this cool and trying to keep me far away from the investigation. But he didn't know what I knew, and I wasn't going to share it with him. Not yet, at least. Mostly because I knew what his response would be: stay away.

He slid out of the booth. "Enjoy your carrot pudding."

I wished I didn't feel so deflated after he left. But I did.

"Get that look out of your eyes," Jamie said.

"What look?"

"The puppy that just lost her home look."

I laughed—quickly, sarcastically—and sarcasm was never becoming. It was a defense mechanism right now, though. "Don't be ridiculous."

"At least you have Drew now to distract you."

"I'm not sure that's a good reason to ever date anyone. Drew deserves to be more than a distraction."

"Don't overthink this. Just get to know him. I have a feeling your thoughts will be more on him than on Chase, after all."

"You think?"

She nodded. "I think."

***

This morning, I sat at work and tried to focus. I was having a hard time.

Instead, I reviewed what I knew—or didn't know, for that matter. The three employees Jamie and I had talked to at Bombay Joe's last night didn't appear to know anything. Or, more likely, Chase had told them on the way out not to talk to us. Which would explain his quiet conversation and pointed look while chatting with the manager.

In other words, I'd eaten carrot pudding for nothing.

Every lead seemed to be drying up.

At ten, I was informed that I had someone who wanted to see me. I looked up and spotted a man and woman I didn't recognize. She was tall with big blonde hair and heavy eye makeup. The man was short with thinning hair and a suit that looked about twenty years old.

I directed them to a conference room, deciding that privacy was a great option here since I had no idea what to expect from this conversation. I'd had some doozies during my tenure working for Ralph.

As soon as I closed the door, the woman threw her arms around me and sobbed into my hair. I stiffened.

What in the world was going on? With a touch of hesitation, I reluctantly patted her back.

"Oh, Holly," she said, stepping back and wiping the tears from beneath her eyes. "I'm so happy to finally meet. I just wish it wasn't under these circumstances."

I had no idea what circumstances she was talking about.

No sooner had she released me than the man also pulled me into a hug.

"I just can't believe he's gone," he muttered.

Were they talking about . . . Travis?

When the man pulled away, the couple both stood there and stared at me with tears in their eyes. They were obviously waiting for my reaction, for my response, and for things to magically click into place in my mind.

I'd never felt so awkward in my life.

"I . . . uh . . ." What did I even say? "You are . . . ?"

The woman waved a hand in the air. "I'm so sorry. I know you're probably overwhelmed and not thinking clearly. I know we are also. But we've heard so much about you that we feel like we know you."

"Is that right?" I was still trying to piece this all together but with no luck.

"We're Travis's parents," the man said. "Mr. and Mrs. Hooker. Or you can just call us Mom and Dad."

My stomach dropped. This was not good. Not good at all.

"I think there might be a misunderstanding—"

"He was head over heels in love with you," Mama Hooker said, clasping her hands beneath her chin. "Couldn't say enough good things about his Holly Bear."

Facts began settling in my mind like a doomsday checklist, and I desperately wanted to be anywhere but here having this conversation. "Travis even told you I worked here, huh?"

Which was weird since I'd never told Travis that.

This whole mystery deepened.

"Oh, yes," Papa Hooker said. "He was so proud of you. He always talked about all the mysteries you were solving."

How in the world had he known that? I had helped to solve a few mysteries in the past, but it wasn't exactly common knowledge.

Mama Hooker sniffled and ran a lacy handkerchief beneath her eyes. "Which is just one more reason why we had to find you here today. You meant so much to him. Because of that, you mean so much to us also."

This was getting worse instead of better. "But—"

Mama Hooker straightened and squeezed my shoulder. "We're having a luncheon for all of Travis's friends today. I'm so glad we were able to find you. Your number is unlisted! We didn't think we'd ever find you, so we just came here on a whim."

"My apologies that it was such a headache in an already difficult time," I said, wondering about the wisdom of my words.

"Oh, go figure you'd say something so sweet when you have to be hurting so much." Mama Hooker hugged me again. "We're meeting at Travis's favorite restaurant to commemorate him in an hour and a half. You'll be there won't you?"

I released my pent up breath and forced a smile. "I wouldn't miss it."

***

There were several problems I faced after that conversation, starting with the fact that I had no idea what Travis's favorite restaurant was. Then there was the fact that I'd never even met Travis face-to-face. But he'd obviously researched me, a factor that made me more than a little uneasy.

Had he purposefully picked me out on that dating site? But why? And how was I going to break the news to his grieving family that we weren't dating?

I searched my memories for any hints that he may have given in our online conversations as to where he liked to eat. Had he mentioned a restaurant?

The Yellow Turtle.

That's where we were supposed to eat that night. Could it be because it was his favorite place?

I made a quick call and asked if there was a large reservation at noon. The hostess confirmed there was.

That had to be the place.

I could hardly concentrate as I tried to squeeze some work in. Finally, I grabbed my purse. I was going to the luncheon, and I would walk there since it was only a few blocks away.

As anxiety built in me, I knew I needed to hash this out with someone before I arrived. Thankfully, Jamie answered the phone, and I poured it all out to her.

"For real? This would only happen to you, Holly." She snorted, sounding way too entertained by this. "What are you going to do, girl?"

I remembered the hopeful look on their faces. "I have no idea. I have to let them know that we weren't really dating. I just don't have the heart to burst their bubble in the middle of their grief."

"And that's just one more thing to love about you."

I dodged crowds of other professionals who were also out seeking a place to eat on the sunny day. Something else was bothering me, I realized. Really bothering me. "I just don't understand how Travis had all this information on me."

"Things aren't what they seemed, are they?"

"No, they're not." I stopped in front of the restaurant and frowned as I faced this dreadful task. "Okay, I've got to go. I'm here."

"Let me know what happens. This is more entertaining than watching reruns of *Scandal*."

***

I walked into The Yellow Turtle and paused. The scent of fried chicken and other home-style foods teased me. This place was downhome with a modern twist. I scanned the dining area and saw a crowd had gathered in a back room.

That must be the Hooker party.

As I stepped that way, the first person I saw was Drew. Our gazes met, and I shrugged apologetically.

How was I going to explain this?

I could kiss any future with him goodbye.

Before I could make my way toward him, the Hookers found me and gave me big bear hugs again. They acted like I was a long-lost daughter.

I couldn't tell them right now, especially since they already had so much grief.

As a waitress interrupted to chat with them about lunch, I scanned the room again. I didn't know anyone else here besides Drew. But I did recognize Ronald Dillow from the photo I'd seen online. Interesting that he'd come, especially considering the allegations against him. I needed to talk to him.

"Okay, everyone!" Mama Hooker said, clapping her hands. "We went ahead and ordered a buffet lunch for everyone. Come and eat. I've also brought pictures of Travis so we can all remember him. Please feel free to take a look. I've left them on the table in the corner. It means so much that you'd all be here right now to remember my sweet boy." Her voice caught.

Poor woman. I couldn't imagine what it would be like to lose a son. Losing a father had been hard enough.

I edged toward the buffet line, which was already full. As I passed the photos, I stopped cold.

There were pictures of Travis. And me. Lots of them. Pictures of us as the sun set behind us with silhouettes of palm trees. Another of us with a snowy mountain in the background. Still another one of us at the park . . . it was just like the picture of Chase and I at the park, only instead of Chase, it was Travis's face.

What . . . ?

He must have digitally altered them.

My mouth dropped open.

"So . . ." someone said behind me.

I turned and saw Drew staring at the pictures. His hands were stuffed in his pockets and a melancholy expression captured his face.

"This is weird," I started.

"You could have just told me if you were dating Travis," he said quietly. "I would have been okay with that."

"I never met Travis," I whispered. "I told you the truth."

He narrowed his eyes with doubt and nodded toward the pictures. Questions lingered in his gaze.

"They were photoshopped. That's the only way to explain it."

He still looked unconvinced. "Then why are you here?"

I leaned closer. "Apparently, Travis told his parents we were dating. They tracked me down at work—because I guess Travis knew where I worked and told them—and insisted I come."

His eyes widened. "You didn't correct them?"

"I could hardly get a word in."

"But you came anyway?"

I shrugged.

"You're one interesting lady, Holly Paladin."

I crossed my arms. "I never set out to be interesting."

"And that only makes you even more interesting." He offered a soft smile.

Just then, the Hookers joined me again.

"Drew, I suppose you already know Travis's girlfriend, Holly," Mama Hooker said. "We can't tell you how happy we were that he finally met such a nice girl. It gives us such comfort to know he was happy in his final days."

I offered a weak smile and looked at Drew.

A mix of amusement and compassion mingled in his

gaze.

This was going to be interesting.

***

I decided to forgo eating. Instead, I would mingle and try to dig up some information.

Someone had cornered Drew. Based on the man's body language, I couldn't imagine Drew getting away any time soon. Maybe that was for the best. I couldn't appear too buddy-buddy with Drew when the Hookers thought I'd been dating their son.

What a mess.

I needed to fix it. Sometime. But maybe I'd let them have their moment now.

Instead, I spotted Ronald Dillow across the room, standing by himself. This was my opportunity.

"You're Travis's girlfriend, right?" he said. "I saw the pictures. That son of a gun never even told me he'd found someone to go steady with."

He jangled his keys in his pockets. The man looked uncomfortable, at best; like an outcast, at worst.

"It's complicated."

Ronald laughed—the sound loud, clipped, and amused. "It always was with Travis."

"You were his boss?"

He nodded, looking around the room with a strange look in his eyes. "That's right. I'm apparently also a suspect. That's probably why no one here is really talking to me."

"I'm sorry." Was that the right thing to say? Or

should I look horrified? I decided to keep it real. "Why would people think you're a suspect?"

"Travis and I . . . we'd had some disagreements lately." He shifted, his level of discomfort obviously skyrocketing.

"What about?"

"Stuff that would bore you. But, long story short, I expect my employees to honor my good name. It's no different than Drew Williams's philosophy. He feels very firmly that reputation is everything in this business. Some people complained about Travis. Said his gaze was shifty at their houses and that made them uncomfortable."

"I see."

"Another man said he caught Travis going through his dead wife's lingerie drawer." Ron wiped the sweat from his head. "As you can imagine, that wasn't a fun discussion."

That would be Dr. Dan Gilbert.

"I'm kind of surprised you didn't fire him." I watched his reaction.

He wiped his forehead again. "I tried to. But he said he was turning things around. That he'd gone through a rough patch, but that was going to change."

Interesting. "Do you have any idea what that meant?"

He shook his head. "No idea. But things weren't turning around. He was acting as strange as ever lately. Not to speak poorly of the dead, but his death has put a strain on us—all of us, from my business to Wilford Funeral Home. I've worked with that family for a long time, and I hate to see good people's names run through the mud."

I stepped closer, turning so my back was no longer toward the room. I wanted to watch the crowd. "So, do you have any idea who might have wanted him dead? I've hardly been able to sleep thinking about it. I've been having nightmares, for that matter."

"Not really," he said. "But I did overhear a nasty fight between Travis and Raul."

"Raul?" There was a name I hadn't heard before.

Ronald nodded at someone in the distance. "It's Drew's brother. If I were the police, he'd be the one I'd look at."

CHAPTER 11

A few minutes later, Drew finally got away from the man who was talking his ear off. He introduced me to other people who worked with Wilford Funeral Home. I welcomed the break from the ever-attentive Hookers, who'd now latched onto one of Travis's aunts who'd just shown up.

After Drew introduced me around, his brother pulled him to the side to talk about something. I kept my eyes on them while trying to make small talk. Raul looked a lot like his brother, but he was taller and thicker, and his eyes weren't as kind. What could he and Travis have been arguing over? I'd hate to point the finger at one of Drew's relatives, but I needed to keep my eyes open.

"I still can't believe Travis is gone," the woman beside me said.

The twentysomething woman named Alicia worked as a receptionist at Wilford Funeral Home. She was probably around my height with light brown hair cut to her shoulders and pixie-like features.

She'd be a good person to know because

receptionists, in my experience, seemed to know a lot about what went on around the office.

Another was a man named AJ, and I could tell he and Drew were good friends from their banter. I'd guess him to be five eight. He had blond hair and a hipster vibe, with his suspenders and bow tie. He worked some kind of career within the death industry. He either was a rep for an organ donation company or a casket company. I'd tuned out part of the conversation, unfortunately.

"We're all in shock," AJ said. "It's hard to believe we were playing basketball just last week."

"He was just talking about buying a house," Alicia said. "A nice one. It was going to be like a trophy to him. That was so Travis."

"He'll be missed," AJ said.

Silence fell for a minute, and I could feel their eyes on me.

"I hope this doesn't sound rude, but I didn't realize Travis was dating anyone." Alicia stared at me, curiosity on her face.

And here I went again. "It's complicated."

She nodded as if fully accepting that answer. "I get that."

I needed to play this for all I could. Maybe it was wrong, but right now I had their sympathies.

"What I can't figure out is why someone would kill him." I shook my head, still fishing for information. "It just makes no sense."

"That's been all I can think about also," Alicia said, lowering her voice. "Who would do something like this?"

"Maybe it's that doctor who was so mad at him," AJ said. "Travis said the man was threatening him, coming by his house even."

Dan Gilbert.

"I heard the police talked to that guy, and he had an alibi for the time of the murder," I said. When they stared at me longer, I shrugged. "I asked when they were questioning me. Apparently, the police question everyone connected with the victim in a case like this."

They both seemed to accept that answer and nodded.

AJ stepped closer. "While we're theorizing, some people have pointed to Ronald over there."

"What do you think of that?" I asked quietly.

"I'm not sure," AJ said. "He's always seemed like an upright guy to me. But do we really know people? Maybe their issues went deeper than I thought."

"You're saying he has no motive?" I asked. "I heard Travis and Ronald argued a lot. Any idea what that was about?"

AJ shook his head. "No idea. Could just be work life in general. The job can be stressful, and not everyone is cut out for it."

"I hope the police will figure it out." I stepped closer. "What about Raul? I heard he and Travis had some issues. Do you know if the police are looking into him?"

AJ's eyebrows shot up. "Raul? Really? I don't know what to say. He does work for a medical supply company, so he'd have access to the supplies needed to poison someone—if that's really what happened. It's all a rumor right now."

Interesting.

"There's one other thing that's been bugging me," Alicia whispered. "Travis seemed to legitimately come into some money lately. I don't know where it came from. His job didn't pay him that well."

Another very interesting fact. These two were full of information. "Why do you say he came into some money?"

"He told me that debt collectors were going to be a thing of his past," Alicia said.

"You think he was doing something illegal on the side?" I whispered.

She frowned and shrugged. "I hate to talk ill of the dead, but maybe. Otherwise, it just makes no sense. But there were a lot of things that didn't make sense about Travis. Some things, I guess we'll never understand this side of heaven. He took his secrets with him to the grave."

Before we could talk anymore, the Hookers joined us. Mama Hooker took my arm, ready to introduce me to more people as the love of Travis's life.

As she did, my phone buzzed again. I sneaked a look at it and my muscles went stiff.

I know what you're doing. Your time is coming. First opportunity and you'll meet Travis . . . in the afterlife this time.

***

I went back to work for a few hours, then stopped by the youth center where I volunteered. After dinner, I stared at the card with Drew Williams's information on it.

Tonight was Bible study. Should I go or should I stay home?

I wasn't sure.

But the thought of returning to my empty home wasn't appealing.

With that in mind, I headed toward Drew's. There in the driveway was his cherry-red Mustang. The police must have already processed it and given it back to him.

A million doubts clashed in my mind as I walked up to the front door. What if I felt uncomfortable and awkward inside? What if everyone assumed I was Drew's date? Again—awkward. What if I had nothing in common with anyone here and felt like an outsider?

There were three other cars outside also. I could hear happy voices drifting from the interior. That was a good sign . . . right?

Bible study sounded great after a day like today. I still couldn't get the Hookers out of my mind. They just seemed to like me so much, and I hadn't had the heart to break it to them that I'd never even met their son. When I'd left the luncheon, they'd handed me their number and asked me to be in touch. Like a robot, I'd nodded and said okay.

I knocked at the door. My breathing was much more shallow than it should have been as I stood there. I'd never thought of myself as one to get social anxiety, but maybe I was.

In fact, maybe this was a terrible idea.

I turned to flee back to my car. Obviously, no one

had heard the doorbell. I could leave now, and no one would be the wiser for it.

Just as my shoe hit the top step, the door opened behind me. I froze and slowly turned around, realizing the only thing worse than feeling awkward *during* a Bible study was feeling awkward *before* the Bible study when you're caught trying to run away.

Drew stood there with a smile stretched across his face. "Holly, you came. I'm so glad."

I raised the plate of cookies I'd brought with me. I'd baked them with my girls at the youth center earlier. "I bring good news of great joy."

He raised an eyebrow. "Come again?"

"That's what the cookies are called. Good news of great joy. I've been waiting to use that line for a long time."

He chuckled. "We always accept food, with special priority given to those with biblical references."

"That's what I was hoping. If the biblical name doesn't win people over, maybe the chocolate and caramel will."

"You had me at cookies." He took the plate and smiled again. "Please, come in. I was hoping you'd show up."

I stepped into his home. I'd already studied the outside of his neat two-story, brick house, and I'd been impressed. The inside didn't disappoint—it was decorated just as neatly. Glossy wood floors, classic furnishings, clean lines. Not too many accessories, but just enough to make it warm.

"Nice place," I said.

He looked behind him. "I can't take any credit for it. My mom helped. So did my sister."

"Well, they did a good job."

"I'll let them know." He took my arm. "Come meet everyone."

Another quell of nerves rose in me. But when I stepped into the living room, I recognized two faces from church. Both of those ladies came over and gave me a huge hug. As soon as their arms wrapped around me, the tension in my muscles eased.

Coming here had been the right choice.

This is it, Holly. This is you. Moving on.

CHAPTER 12

The Bible study was all about trusting that God was in control—living it out, putting it into action, and not just talking the talk. It had been just what I needed to be reminded of. Coming here had been the right choice, despite all of my insecurities.

And, somehow, I ended up being the last one to leave. Probably because I'd offered to help straighten up. After all, it was the polite thing to do, and Drew seemed to appreciate the help.

When I put the last dish into the dishwasher, I found my purse and turned toward Drew. A rush of nerves rippled through me as we stood in front of each other. "I should run."

He stepped closer, and his sandalwood scent surrounded me. His eyes were warm on mine and that ever-ready smile present. He was smooth and gentle, yet he'd taken charge of the conversation at Bible study, keeping the group focused on the topic. He'd made everyone feel welcome, yet he still gave off a masculine vibe. I'd been impressed.

He stuffed his hands deep into his pockets. "I'm glad you came, Holly."

"Thanks for inviting me." I walked slowly toward the door, Drew shadowing my steps, and we paused.

"Holly?"

I turned. "Yes?"

"Do you want to have dinner tomorrow night?"

I hesitated but only for a minute. I'd been kind of hoping that he'd ask, and I had no good reason to say no. "Yes, I'd love to."

His grin stretched wider. "Great. I'll call you with details—if you'd be as kind as to pass on your number. Would that work?"

"I'd be more than happy to." I rattled off my number, and Drew typed it into his phone. "I look forward to it. Good night, Drew."

"Good night."

I felt myself beaming—just a little, at least—as I left. Drew seemed too good to be true. I had to remind myself that if something seemed too good to be true, it probably was.

But not always. Certainly, there was hope for a few nearly perfect things in this world.

I paused when I got into my car and checked my cell phone. I held my breath, waiting to see if I'd gotten any more texts.

Nothing.

I released the air from my lungs.

Maybe the man had backed off. After all, he had no reason to come after me. I knew nothing.

Yet he seemed to think I did. Or that I had something that I didn't, at least.

As I scrolled through my screen, I saw that I'd

missed three calls and none had left voicemails.

I squinted at one of the numbers. Who was that?

The number seemed strangely familiar, yet I couldn't place it.

I didn't usually call unknown numbers back, but I decided to this time. I locked my door—just to be safe—and listened to the phone ring.

As I waited, I glanced around, a feeling of unease washing over me again. Why did I constantly feel like someone was watching me? Was it Drew? Had he walked to the door and waited to see if I'd get home safely?

Or maybe it was the sender of those texts. Would he carry out his threat? Did he still believe that I knew more than I actually did?

I glanced at Drew's house. I didn't see him peering from any windows or doors.

I swallowed hard, wondering if it was a good idea to remain in my car unmoving. Just as I cranked the engine, a woman answered.

"Holly?"

"Speaking," I said, trying to place her semi-familiar voice.

"It's Blake."

Blake. I hadn't expected to hear from her so soon. "Blake. How are you?"

"I'm in a bit of a pickle." Her voice shook with uncertainty.

"What's going on?" Still unable to escape the feeling of being watched, I eased down the road, hoping a change of location would make me feel better, safer.

"Like I told you yesterday, I don't know very many people in this area," she started. "I hope you don't mind me calling. You just seem so . . . trustworthy. It's like I feel a kindred bond with you and instinctively know we could be related."

I'd felt that also.

"Anyway, the house I was renting had a water leak we discovered on Friday," she continued. "The contractors came in today and said there's black mold everywhere. I had to move out for health purposes, and I'm looking for a new place to stay. I called a couple people I've met at school, but none of them have an extra room at their places. Most of them live in apartments. You know, we're all poor college students. I was hoping you had some recommendations of someone who might be looking for a last-minute tenant."

I quickly ran through a mental list of anyone I might know who fit the bill. I had no good ideas, unfortunately. I merged onto one of the main traffic arteries that led through my area of town, glancing in the rearview mirror.

I didn't see anyone following me. And, yes, I was looking.

"Off the top of my head, I can't think of anyone," I said. "Have you looked around at some apartment complexes? Maybe there are some openings."

"I tried that. Most people don't want someone who's only going to be there for a month. The rest are too expensive." She let out a sigh. "It's okay. I just thought you might have some recommendations since you had so many connections in the area. Long shot, right?"

Guilt sank into me. I didn't know what I'd do if I didn't have family in the area to help me out when I needed it. Everyone needed a support system. "That stinks about the mold."

"I agree. It was so unexpected." She paused. "Well, I'm sorry to bother you, Holly. Let me make some more phone calls."

Do something, Holly. She's family.

Maybe she's family.

Still, I hesitated a moment. Then I remembered our Bible study tonight. We'd talked about living out the belief that God was in control and acting out of faith instead of fear.

God didn't call me to live a life of comfort but a life of service. It was so easy to forget that. Faith was something you lived out, it wasn't just talking points to recite. Wasn't that what the Bible was about?

"You know what?" I started. "I have an extra bedroom. Why don't you stay with me until you can figure something else out?"

"I'd hate to impose on you."

"You're not."

"Are you sure?"

"Absolutely." I rattled off my address, and she told me she'd be over in an hour.

Pushing myself out of my comfort zone. That's what I was doing. I just hoped I didn't regret it, especially in light of everything that was going on lately.

***

"What do you mean a stranger is moving in with you?" Jamie said.

She'd called right after I hung up with Blake. She already knew the whole story about my supposed cousin, and she'd been a tad skeptical when she heard the details.

"It's not a big deal." I shoved the phone under my ear so I could turn my windshield wipers on.

A light rain had begun to fall. Thankfully, I was almost home. Driving the Mustang during a downpour wasn't my favorite thing. While there were many things classic cars had in their favor, there were other things they didn't have—like anti-lock brakes.

"Of course it is," Jamie said. "Letting someone in your home isn't to be taken lightly."

I glanced behind me once more, making sure no one was there. As far as I could tell, I was good. But it was dark outside, and everyone's headlights were glaring. It was hard to tell one car from another. Maybe I'd just been paranoid earlier.

"I appreciate your concern," I told Jamie. "But Blake is family."

"She's family you just met, and her blood relation hasn't been confirmed. What if she's faking it?"

Her words made me pause. "Why would she do that?"

"Who knows? There are crazy people in this world."

My head was starting to pound now. Why was it that the moment I started to try to act out of faith not fear that someone was certain to point out I was wrong?

"Yes, there are crazy people. You're crazy sometimes."

"It's usually your idea."

"You're not going to get any argument from me there. But can we change the subject? I've already invited her. I can't exactly turn her away now."

"Have you considered she might be connected to this Travis guy? You know, the one who's dead? I mean, the timing of her arrival is suspect. And did you find out who posted on those adoption boards? I still can't see your mom doing that."

"I don't even know where to start after everything you just said," I muttered. "So maybe I won't start. Just let it be known that I heard you."

Jamie let out a sigh, and I could tell she wanted to say more. "Okay, fine. Are you up for going on another date on Friday?"

I wanted to snort. "Um . . . let me think. No. Absolutely not. I took down my profile from that site."

"Why'd you do that?"

"Do you not remember the events of Saturday night?" I gripped the steering wheel tighter as the downpour thickened.

"How could I forget? But that was isolated. Unrelated. It's not like something like that would happen again."

"I'm out, Jamie. I'm sorry. I know we promised to double date, but I just can't do it again. The first time, Travis died. The next time I might be dating a serial killer, for all I know."

"Or he could be Prince Charming."

"Or he could be a serial killer disguised as Prince

Charming." Drew's face flashed into my mind, but I pushed the image away. No way.

Jamie laughed. "Okay, okay. I get it."

"Besides, I kind of have a date this week." I'd been contemplating whether or not I should share.

She remained quiet a moment, as if I'd thrown her off balance. "Kind of? Either you do or you don't."

"Okay, I do." I smiled when I remembered my conversation with Drew—who wasn't a serial killer.

"With . . . "

"Drew Williams."

She sucked in a breath. "Is that right? Now that's an idea that I could get used to. Please tell me more."

I quickly replayed this evening. "Well, he invited me to Bible study tonight."

"Okay . . ."

"And I went. And I had a good time. And I think he's really nice."

"Really nice is a good start. He's also good-looking."

I pulled into my driveway just in time to start ticking things off on my fingers. "He's got a steady job, a nice house. He's involved at church. He loves God. There's really not anything about him that I shouldn't like."

"I'm proud of you, Holly." Her tone changed from excited to sincere. "You haven't been yourself for the past few months. Maybe you're coming out of that funk finally."

"That's right. Maybe." I cut my engine and listened to the rain patter on my windshield for a moment. "I'm home now, Jamie. I should go."

"Dinner Wednesday night?"

"Dinner Wednesday night. It's confirmed." We usually met once a week for dinner and to catch up. My times with Jamie were some of my favorite times during the week. Every woman needed a girlfriend like Jamie in their lives—someone she could share everything with, and occasionally be a partner in crime.

"Great. I'll see you then. Until then, sleep with your door locked tonight."

"Very funny."

"Girl, I'm not joking."

CHAPTER 13

I'd barely put my purse down—in my room, of course, because I wasn't *that* trusting—when my doorbell rang.

Blake stood there with a lopsided grin on her face. She looked similar to what she did before. Same basic tight outfit. Nose ring. Hair that looked amazingly like mine.

I was doing the right thing, I told myself. Blake needed someone, and I was here. Why shouldn't I help her? I didn't care what Jamie said. I had no reason not to trust Blake.

But, if that was the truth, why hadn't I informed my family yet? I told myself it was because I wanted to wait until my mom returned, so then I could tell everyone at once. But was that really it?

And what if I was putting Blake in danger by letting her stay here? After all, I was obviously someone's target. Danger seemed to be tailing me. I'd made dangerous people mad, though I had no clue how.

That was the reason I'd told my caseworker that I couldn't take any more foster kids for the time being. I had to get this cleared up first.

"Thank you so much for letting me come over," Blake said as she stepped inside carrying a backpack, two suitcases, and an oversized purse. "It means so much to me."

"No problem." I took one of her bags. "Let me show you to your room."

She followed me down the hallway. This place had three bedrooms. One was mine. The other two I'd designed with foster children in mine. The first had twin beds, one on each side. The other had a double bed in the center of the room. Each was decorated in soft, calming colors.

Children who'd been through trauma needed as much help calming them down as possible. Some people might think these were just paint colors, but to me, they were one more method of therapy, a way of promoting peace and calm.

"You have kids?" Blake dropped her bag onto the double bed and stared at the room.

"No, but I'm a foster mom."

Her eyebrows shot up. "Are you? That's wonderful."

"It's something I've always wanted to do." And I had. Ever since I saw the heartache those kids went through while in my role as social worker, I'd known I was meant to do this. I thought I needed to wait until I was married, but that wasn't true at all. The time was now for living my dreams, with or without a man by my side.

"More power to you." Her expression turned serious. "I know I already said this, but you can't imagine how much I appreciate this."

"It's really no problem. Can I get you anything? Some

tea maybe?"

"If it's okay, I'm super tired. Is it alright if I turn in for the night? I had such a long day, and I'm exhausted. I've got to study a little before I go to bed also. Big test tomorrow."

That was actually fine with me. I needed some time to decompress and sort through all my thoughts. I'd even considered doing some research on Travis's boss, to see if he could be the guy who was threatening me.

Then again, I hadn't received any more angry texts. Maybe I could finally put all of this behind me.

"That's no problem. I'm pretty tired myself." I paused before leaving her room. "I have a meeting early in the morning, so I may be gone when you wake up. I'll leave an extra key on the kitchen counter. Help yourself to any food in the house."

"That's perfect. I have class at nine, and I'll be gone most of the day."

"Have a good night." I closed the door, suddenly uneasy.

It was nothing, I told myself. Just Jamie putting ideas in my head. Blake was harmless. I could envision her becoming like the little sister I'd never had. After all, we seemed to have a lot in common. We were possibly blood related even.

And besides, I had strangers stay in my house all the time. Granted, they were usually six-, seven-, and eight-year-olds. But there was nothing weird about this.

I was going to prove Jamie wrong.

***

I tossed and turned in bed, and I wasn't sure why.

Maybe it had something to do with the fact that I'd locked my bedroom door, and then gotten up to unlock it, chiding myself about being paranoid, then I'd locked it again just to be on the safe side. And then I'd unlocked it.

It was a lesson in futility.

I'd finally left it unlocked, but now I wasn't sleeping well.

Then I heard a creak.

My entire body tensed.

I was hearing things. That had to be it. Or the house was settling. I hadn't lived here for long enough to learn all the sounds. Or Blake had gotten up to go to the bathroom.

That was probably it. Of course.

I nearly laughed at myself for being so suspicious.

Despite that realization, another creak made my blood go ice cold.

That did it. I needed to check out that sound. And lock the bedroom door once and for all.

I started to push myself up and face the dark room, to lose the comfort of the fluffy blanket that offered a strange security. Before I'd even raised my head, a hand pressed against my mouth. A figure in black pounced on top of me. My muscles went ramrod straight.

"I'm sorry he had to drag you into this," a gruff voice said. "Holly Paladin."

What in the world was he talking about? What was I missing? I needed to fight, to try and get away. Instead, I froze, my thoughts incoherent.

"I'm going to move my hand, but if you scream or alert anyone that I'm here, I'll kill you." The sharp edge of his voice left no room for doubt.

My heart pounded in my ears. I stared at him. He wore a ski mask. Had colorless eyes. The rest of his body was covered, blending in with the night and offering no clues to his identity.

"Do you understand?" he repeated, pressing his hand harder over my mouth.

I nodded, my fluffy pillow surrounding my head. Encasing it. Suffocating me.

Slowly, the intruder released his gloved hand from my lips. "Now, let's make this easy before I kill you. Where is it?"

"I don't know what you're talking about." My voice came out at a high-pitched squeak, nearly indecipherable, even to my own ears.

He growled and leered closer. "Don't play stupid. Tell me where the information is. I know he slipped it to you."

My mind raced as pieces clicked together. "What information? Who slipped it to me?"

"Stop playing stupid. I'm losing my patience with you. If the police had the info, I'd be in jail right now."

Another jolt of fear seized me. "I found a key and gave it to the police. I didn't know where it came from. Is that the information?"

The man muttered something not nice beneath his breath. Then he raised a syringe and brought it to my throat, devilishly aiming the sharp metallic point at my skin. I held my breath, afraid to breathe. Breathing was moving. Moving even one-eighth of an inch could send the needle into my neck.

"Where's the rest of it?"

The blood drained from my head so quickly that I feared I might pass out. "I have no idea what you're talking about."

He dragged the tip of the syringe against my neck as if picturing the sadistic act of watching me die. "I'd hate to inject this too slowly—so slowly that you die a long, prolonged death. I made it easy on Travis. One injection, and he was dead a couple minutes later."

I held my breath and waited, each second crawling by as I waited to see what the man would do next.

"I guess my work here is done," he whispered. "Sorry that you're collateral damage."

He raised the syringe but, as he did, a creak sounded in the hallway.

The man stiffened.

"You're not alone?" he whispered.

I shook my head, at once thankful that Blake was here. But I hoped she didn't walk in my room right now and get herself in trouble.

As quickly as the man appeared, he jumped away and ran toward the window.

"This isn't over," he mumbled.

And then he opened the window, shoved out the screen, and he was gone.

I froze, unable to move. My heart still raced out of control and my head spun.

But I was wasting time. These moments after a

crime were vital.

With trembling limbs, I grabbed my phone from the nightstand and called Chase. He promised to be right over.

Then I ran into the hallway. Blake stood there with a dazed expression. I recognized it from one of my foster kids.

She was sleepwalking.

Thankfully, she allowed me to lead her back into her room and into bed. She had no idea any of this had happened. Her presence, however, may have saved my life.

That could have been ugly. I praised God the man had left before things turned deadly.

But what in the world had that man been talking about? What information?

I needed to find out before my ignorance got me killed.

CHAPTER 14

"Chase." The word escaped with a rasp when I saw him standing on the porch.

He stepped toward me, and I had to resist the urge to fall into his arms. I could tell that he had to resist the urge to pull me into an embrace. Instead, an invisible rock separated us, mocking and cruel.

Two uniformed officers rushed in behind him. I skirted to the side to let them do their job, though I had a feeling they wouldn't find any evidence.

"Are you okay?" Chase scooted closer, his voice low and intimate, like he was hugging me even though we weren't touching.

I nodded and rubbed my neck, needing to do something with my hands before I reached for him. Breakup etiquette rule 19: definitely don't touch. I didn't know if that was really a rule or not, but it sounded right.

"I am. Thankfully."

Just then, Chase's gaze traveled behind me, and his eyes narrowed. I turned and saw Blake standing there. Her hair was matted with bedhead. She wore some flannel pajama bottoms with an oversized knit top, and lines from her pillow were still etched into her cheek.

"Holly?" Chase's gaze darted down to me, questions haunting their depths.

I knew exactly what he was thinking: that I'd taken in a stray. He knew me a little too well. And I knew him a little too well, because I knew he wouldn't approve. Not by a long shot.

"This is Blake. It's a long story, but she's staying with me for a while. Blake, this is Chase. He's . . ." What did I say? My ex? No, I couldn't go there. "He's a detective and a friend."

Blake fluttered her hand in the air, and Chase offered a terse nod before taking my arm. He pulled me to the corner of my living room, away from anyone else who could hear what he had to say.

"Who is that girl, Holly?" His voice had an edge to it.

I crossed my arms, bracing myself for this conversation. "She might be a cousin."

A knot formed between his eyes. "What does that mean? *Might* be a cousin?"

"Like I said, it's a long story." And I really didn't want to get into it right now. I'd already had one doozy of a night, and this conversation was only upping my stress level into the stratosphere.

He shifted and ran a hand over his face in what was clearly exasperation personified. "What do you know about her?"

I raised my chin. "Enough."

"I doubt that. How do you know she doesn't have anything to do with this?"

"That's ridiculous." I lowered my voice once I

realized it was rising. But what Chase was suggesting was ludicrous. Why would Blake help someone threaten me? Someone could do that on their own.

Chase leaned closer. "There's no sign of forced entry."

"You think she let someone in?"

"It's a possibility."

"I repeat: that's ridiculous." I refused to believe his theory. I wouldn't even entertain it. Not right now, at least.

"Maybe you need to rethink your choice."

"I can make my own choices." I raised my chin even higher, so tired of people telling me what to do. Why did people feel the need to take care of me? Did I give off a desperate vibe or something? Whatever it was, it needed to change. Pronto.

"Of course you can." Chase's jaw flexed. "I just hope those choices don't get you killed."

I was moving beyond testiness at this conversation and headed straight toward being offended. I lowered my voice as I barked out, "You and Jamie both must think I'm incapable of using wisdom or common sense."

His jaw flexed. "I didn't say that. I just know you have a good heart that other people could take advantage of. Not everyone has pure intentions like you do."

"I appreciate the heads up, but I'll be fine."

He gave me one last smoldering stare before taking another step back. "Let me go check out things and touch base with the officers."

"Chase," I called, remembering the key and the

subsequent threats that may or may not be related to them. I'd had something on my mind before the conversation took this turn.

He paused. "Yes?"

"Did you find out anything about that key that was in my pocket?"

His gaze darkened. "No, we still don't know much about it. It's a house key, best we can tell. We don't know which house, and, frankly, I'm not sure we'll ever know."

But a house key just didn't make sense to me. "Why would someone go through all of this trouble for a house key? Couldn't they just pick the lock? Kick the door down?"

"That's what we're trying to figure out."

Apparently, that's what I needed to figure out also. I knew there was no way to get that key back from Chase. I'd be foolish to try. That meant I needed to find answers before the killer could find me again.

"There's one other thing you should know," Chase said. "We've arrested someone for Travis's murder."

I sucked in a quick breath. "Who?"

"Ronald Dillow."

"I met him earlier when I was talking to the Hookers."

Chase's jaw dropped. "Why were you talking to prostitutes?"

"Not prostitutes. Travis's family," I explained. "Anyway, did he confess?"

Chase shook his head. "But he's got motive. He was angry with Travis for some of his work habits, and he actually said that Travis was going to end up being one of his clients—a dead body that needed to be transported."

"So, what you're saying is that the person you think murdered Travis is behind bars, so he's not the same person who broke in tonight?" Was I understanding this correctly?

"That's how it appears."

"But this guy said he killed Travis. He had a syringe."

"This definitely makes us look at the case in a new light."

Were there two bad guys here? Were they working together?

Because based on what I understood after this evening, the real killer was still out there.

***

Despite everything that had happened, I decided to keep my plans for the next morning. Breakfast with my brother and sister might just be the distraction I needed. Otherwise, last night's events might consume my thoughts, and I didn't want that to happen.

Blake had confessed last night that she could have unlocked the door while sleepwalking and that she'd been known to do so in the past. She'd apologized a million times, and I had no good reason not to believe her. However, my confidence in my choice to let her stay with me was waning.

The whole situation surrounding Travis also had me on edge. Every time I got a text, I felt anxiety trying to swallow me. When would the man strike again? What would he do next time? How was I going to find answers?

Since I couldn't sleep after all the excitement last night, I'd spent my time making coffee cake, cranberry muffins, and a cream cheese danish. Baking therapy. That's what I called it. When I'd finished those, I'd made some chocolate chip cookies. I left some at the house for Blake, but brought most of what I made with me for the breakfast.

I arrived early to my mom's house—where we always met—so I could make coffee. That was my role, it seemed. I liked being the provider of tasty treats that nurtured the stomach and the soul. That might seem insignificant or frivolous to some people, but I loved it.

I'd just finished setting the table when Alex and Ralph arrived. Alex was expecting her first baby in three months. She was tall, thin, intelligent, and beautiful. She was also ten years older, and she liked to be in charge of everything and everyone—especially me.

Ralph's wife had died several years ago in an auto accident, only six months into their marriage. He hadn't really looked at anyone since then and seemed content to focus on his work. He'd previously been a high school principal and then a school board member before running for the senate. He was nerdy cute and had a propensity toward sweater vests and plastic-framed glasses. He was eight years older than I, and had also been like another parent to me.

We chitchatted for several minutes about work and schedules and Alex's baby—generic stuff. About fifteen minutes into our conversation, Alex's studious gaze fell on me.

"Why do you seem nervous?" she asked, taking a bite of her coffee cake.

I'd been contemplating all night whether I should share the news about Blake. They were both smart enough to use discernment with the information. Besides, I wanted to know if one of them had placed the ad.

"Someone showed up Sunday claiming to be related to Dad," I started, laying everything on the table.

They both froze and lowered their food and drinks back to the table.

I dove in and told them all I knew.

"You think she's for real?" Alex crossed her arms, her contemplative attorney look claiming each of her facial muscles. "I can run a background check on her."

"She seemed legit." I'd left out the part about her staying at my house. I didn't need another lecture. "Besides, why would someone pretend to be related to us? It's not like we're loaded."

Alex and Ralph both stared at me like I suddenly had a forked tongue.

"You're not serious, right?" Ralph said. "Politics. Court cases. State legislation. There are any number of reasons."

"I can't see her doing that," I said, knowing my argument was futile.

"But you don't know her," Alex said. "You think the best of people."

The way she said it made it clear that she didn't

think that quality was an attribute.

"Don't you want people to think the best about you?" I asked, holding my frustration at bay. Attempting to, at least.

There were some things I'd just never see eye to eye about with my family. I'd been more like my dad, and that was just one more reason I missed him. He'd understood me while no one else in my family seemed to try.

"Of course, but this situation is different." Ralph pushed his glasses up higher on his nose. "This is someone claiming to be related. We need to be diligent."

"Did either of you put the ad in the adoption forum?"

They both stared at me. No, they didn't. That was my answer.

"Why would we do that?" Alex asked.

"Someone did," I said.

"You think Mom did?" Ralph responded.

"If none of us did, then that only leaves Mom."

"That seems so unlike her." Alex sat back and rubbed her pregnant stomach, appearing deep in thought.

"So, what should I tell Blake if we speak again?" I asked, choosing my words carefully. "That I need to wait until she's passed a background check, credit check, and criminal records check?"

"Of course not," Alex scoffed with a half eye roll. "We just need more information."

"For that matter, I would like to meet her," Ralph said. "But we need to be careful how close we let her get. Like, we can't let her into our homes or anything." He laughed, like the idea was ludicrous.

I quickly looked away before they could read the truth in my gaze. I'd had my fill of lectures for the week.

***

I requested to work at home today, which Ralph was totally okay with. I needed to be at my house because I'd hired someone to come in and install a security system. I had to do whatever I could to prevent someone from breaking in and nearly killing me again. Besides, next time this guy might not nearly kill me. He might *actually* kill me.

I shivered at the thought.

The company had come at nine, and it had only taken three hours to install the new system and teach me how to use it. I worked as the security company worked, and then I took a break for lunch.

I stared at my phone, thinking about calling the Hookers, but I decided to delay the inevitable act a little bit longer.

Instead, while munching on some carrots and celery, I did another search for Ronald Dillow and Dillow Mortuary Transportation.

To my surprise, the company had a pretty extensive online presence. I clicked on Ronald's picture and studied it again.

He looked like a nice enough man. Even nice people were capable of murder, however. But I'd met Ronald, and he just didn't strike me as the type to plan something so thoroughly.

Next I clicked on Travis's picture. His bio didn't

contain anything surprising. He was from Columbus. He loved vintage cars. He rooted for the Cincinnati Bengals.

I continued to scroll through the pictures on the Dillow Mortuary Transportation site until I stopped at one.

It was the man—the one who'd run into me Saturday night and left the key in my pocket. He'd been right under my nose the whole time. I'd just never thought to look.

His name was listed as Chuck Rogers.

He looked different in the picture. He didn't have that chinstrap beard or whatever Jamie had called it. But I felt 99 percent certain this was him.

My pulse spiked. I was onto something. Finally!

I grabbed my phone and called Chase.

"Good work, Holly," he muttered. "I'll go see what I can find out."

"Let me go with you," I blurted.

"I don't know if that's a good idea."

"Please."

He remained quiet a moment. "You promise to stay out of this?"

"Of course."

"I'll be there in five. Don't make me regret this. Please."

***

I sat in Chase's car and watched as he approached Chuck's front door.

This could be it. This could be the moment we found

some answers, and I'd be able to put this behind me.

A car sat in the driveway, which led me to believe that Chuck was home. His house was more of a rundown shack with siding that was falling off. The whole place was surrounded by overgrown grass and lots of small trees and shrubs that hadn't been trimmed . . . ever?

As I waited, my mind raced, trying to piece together what I already knew. Chuck hadn't been at the get-together the Hookers had planned. Why was that? His other coworkers were there.

I chewed on that thought. I needed to find out. For now, it only served to cast him in a negative light—a guilty light.

I hummed "You'll Never Walk Alone." It could be my theme song with the lyric's sentiments of holding your head up high through trials. I had to pass my time in the car somehow, and humming a song about keeping me head up high seemed to do the trick.

On the way here, Chase had told me that Dr. Dan Gilbert was MIA. No one had seen him all day. I wondered what that meant.

But right now, I really wanted to know about this guy. Chuck.

Chase knocked on the door again, but no one answered still. I watched as he moved around the house. He peered in the front window. He then moved around the house to another window.

I sensed something change in his demeanor. A sense of urgency emerged, evident in his quickened steps and tight muscles.

He called someone on his phone before rushing toward the front door. Quickly, he tried the knob, but it appeared locked. Using his shoulder, he rammed into the door. Two tries later, the wood cracked and the door opened.

I held my breath. Prayed. Theorized what might be happening.

All I could think of was: Chuck was inside murdering someone. Chase had to stop him.

Two minutes later, two other police cars showed up, as well as an ambulance.

This wasn't good. It wasn't good at all. However, I kept my promise and stayed in the car. I gripped the door handle the whole time, desperately wanting to be a part of the action. But I'd given Chase my word.

Twenty minutes later—twenty long, agonizing moments—Chase climbed back into the driver's seat. He stared straight ahead, making no move to leave. His grim expression only added to my unease.

"You were right," he finally said. "This was Chuck's house."

"What did you find?" Dead bodies? A human smuggling ring? A house full of syringes?

Chase finally looked at me. "We found Chuck, Holly. He's dead."

I swallowed hard, unsure if I'd heard correctly. "Do you know how?"

"It appears he was injected with something . . . just like Travis."

CHAPTER 15

"Why do you keep fidgeting?" Jamie asked me that evening as she pinned a lock of my hair in place.

"Sorry. I'm just a little nervous. On so many different levels."

We stood in my small bathroom, one that still had Pepto Bismol pink tiles on the floor, half of the wall, and in the bathtub's surround. It was on my list of things to change, but for now, I was going to tell people I liked the retro look.

Jamie had come over to help me with a new hairstyle that involved several braids being pinned loosely into a bun. It was a very romantic look, and I needed something to bolster my waning confidence tonight. A snazzy A-line dress with a pretty hairdo could do the trick, but I'd needed assistance.

Blake, apparently, was still at class. I hadn't exactly asked for her schedule, though I kind of wished I had. It would be nice to know when she was coming and going, just for my own sanity.

Sure, I'd told her she could stay here, but I wasn't crazy about her being in my home without me. While there were very few worldly possessions I held dear, the ones I did value, I'd take someone down for. Like my father's old record player and his collection of albums from bygone eras. Or the princess figure my father had whittled for me out of an old stick, one that was now proudly displayed on my glass bookshelf.

"I just have a lot on my mind," I muttered, staring at myself in the mirror.

Jamie paused long enough to peer at my reflection. "You're nervous about this, aren't you?"

"Can you blame me? My almost date with Travis ended with him being dead."

"That's not going to happen again."

Perry Como's *Papa Loves Mambo* crooned in the background, helping me relax ever-so-slightly. Perry was good for that. "Famous last words. Not to mention the fact that someone's trying to kill me."

"That is unnerving."

"My last date had ulterior motives for going out with me, and I'm still not sure what they were."

"You're right. You do have a lot to be nervous about." Jamie placed one more bobby pin in my hair and then stepped back. "There, all done. You look gorgeous."

I glanced in the mirror and felt a rush of satisfaction. The look was very Victorian era—soft and feminine. Though I usually preferred the fifties look, the change was nice.

"It looks good. Thank you, Jamie."

She shrugged dramatically and lifted her palm in the air with false humility. "I'll send you my bill, and, girl, I'm expensive. I'm two dozen gluten-free cookies expensive."

"I can handle that." I grabbed my purse and walked with her toward the door. I was so glad I had a friend like Jamie in my life. "Your friendship is priceless."

"I was just reading Bible verses about friendship. Two are better than one. Iron sharpens iron. A friend loveth—and baketh cookies—at all times."

I smiled. "Really?"

"Okay, not that last one."

"You forgot this one: bad company corrupts good character."

She snorted. "You're not bad company."

"I have almost gotten you killed a few times." I frowned as I remembered last night.

"I don't know what you're talking about. Nor can I believe this Chuck guy is dead."

"I did tell you that Dr. Dan has disappeared, right? Chase found out when he went to check out his alibi for last night."

"And Ronald was already behind bars," Jamie reminded me. "So, he's not behind this either."

"There's something big we're missing," I said.

"We'll figure it out."

"Not if someone kills us first."

"Don't be silly. You're like a cat with nine lives." She paused before we exited my house. "So, you're going to call me and let me know how it goes?"

"Of course."

"Don't do anything I wouldn't do."

I chuckled. "Believe me, I won't. The fact that I'm going on this date is a big step. Mind-blowing."

She squeezed my arm, and her voice turned serious. "I know, and I'm proud of you."

We gave each other a quick hug and said goodbye.

I was officially on my own now.

***

I was meeting Drew across the river in Kentucky. Though he seemed like a gentleman, it was better if he didn't know where I lived. I could only imagine the lectures I'd get about that from my well-meaning inner circle. Drew wanted to surprise me with wherever we were eating and had asked me to meet him in front of a parking garage.

As soon as I pulled into the garage and found a space on an upper level, another Mustang pulled in beside me. Drew waved and grinned from the front seat, his white teeth sparkling even in the dim lighting of the cement box around me.

I climbed out, my heart instantly calming when I saw him.

"Hey, there," I said, edging between my car and the VW Beetle beside me.

"Hello, yourself. You look . . ." He looked me up and down before letting out a low whistle. "Gorgeous. Stunning, for that matter."

I was pretty sure I blushed. "Thank you."

"Shall we?" He offered the crook of his arm.

I rested my hand there, feeling like a lady. It was easily one of my top ten favorite feelings ever. Maybe even top three. "Let's."

I had to admit that Drew was a classy guy. He was dressed to the nines in a suit and tie, his hair was neat, and his shoes were polished. He was the picture of a gentleman.

This very well could be a perfect date—but I shouldn't get my hopes up.

"So, how was your day, Holly?" he asked as we reached an elevator.

I remembered the breakfast with my brother and sister, the break-in during the night, Chuck's death, and my uncertainties about Blake. "It was . . . interesting."

"I look forward to hearing about it over dinner."

I needed to figure out how much I would share. But, for now, I nodded and stepped onto the elevator. "How about you? Have you had a good day?"

"It wasn't very busy, which I suppose is a good thing for the community, right?"

"Seems like it would be." I paused, switching subjects in my mind. "Have you heard any updates on what happened to Travis?"

Had he heard Ronald had been arrested? That Chuck was dead? That was what I really wanted to know.

He shook his head. "I heard a couple of rumors regarding the investigation—but nothing's been substantiated yet."

"I heard Ronald Dillow was arrested."

He tilted his head. "You heard?"

"I did."

"Ronald seems like a nice enough man. And I'm still unclear about why the police think he would do something like this. I just can't see it." He let out a soft breath before adding somberly, "Someone else who worked with Travis was also murdered."

"That's got to shake you up a bit." We stepped off the elevator and started down the busy sidewalk.

"To say the least."

I didn't ask where we were going, but Drew led me down the street and past several small, quaint restaurants.

"So . . ." Drew started, hesitation tinging his voice. "I have a confession."

His words caused me to tense. I'd heard a lot of bad confessions before . . . usually right before someone tried to kill me. "Do you?"

"Don't get scared. It's not that frightening, I promise. I need to confess that I Googled you."

I released my breath. I could handle that confession. "Did you?"

"I saw your awards. The one for Volunteer of the Year for the entire city was very impressive."

"I was honored to receive that."

"But I also saw some news articles about some crimes you'd helped solve." His words hung in the air. "I knew you'd done some stuff, but I had no idea just how much."

I knew he wanted more. Was he testing to see if I was some kind of psychopath who liked inserting myself into dangerous situations? Some people might say yes.

But this was me. I was a package deal, and I didn't want to change to suit other people. I was being the person God had created me to be.

"I like helping people," I finally said. "And it seems I'm continually placed in situations where people need my help. People who are uncomfortable going to the police or people who don't know whom they can trust. I have the means and the connections—sometimes—to help them. So that's what I try to do."

"Sounds dangerous."

I shrugged. "Maybe. But it's like I always say, God never called us to be comfortable. He never even called us to be happy. I feel like my life has a greater purpose than pursuing those things."

I watched his reaction, holding my breath as I waited to see if he understood or not. Not everyone could grasp my mentality. It was counterculture to the world. But I believed it with every ounce of my being. Christ had sacrificed his life for me. I was willing to sacrifice whatever I needed to shine His light in the world.

Drew continued to study me a moment, and my gut twisted tighter. I'd just lost him, hadn't I? He'd decided I was too zealous for his tastes.

It wouldn't be the first time. And I was okay with that. Disappointed, but okay.

Finally, his lip twitched. I waited for a sigh, for him to lean back or nod solemnly as he realized that I truly was sold out for my beliefs.

Instead, a smile cracked his face. "I love that, Holly. I love when people see beyond the temporary and into the eternal. Not many people do."

A surprising—and physical—relief, possibly a burst of joy, swept through me.

He didn't think I was crazy.

"I work with death every day," he said. "I've seen how people store up the treasures of this earth. But we all die, and none of us takes any of that with us. We have a much more important purpose and so little time here in the grand scheme of things."

"Exactly!"

We shared a moment.

"We're here." He opened a glass door and swept his hand toward the inside. "Ladies first."

"Very well." I stepped onto a wooden floor beyond the entrance and paused. "A bookstore?"

It was tiny—probably an eight-by-eight room—and there was no one else here, no one except for a woman wearing a black dress and holding a binder in her hands. She smiled pleasantly at us but said nothing. There wasn't even a cash register, for that matter.

My suspicions rose, but I pushed them down. This wasn't a part of someone's plan to kill me . . . I hoped.

"Books before dinner?" I questioned.

Drew's eyes sparkled, and he winked.

Seeing him wink nearly made my knees go weak.

He leaned toward the woman in black and whispered, "Punch the bag."

Alarm raced through me. What bag? Was *I* the bag? That would be highly insulting, to say the least.

The woman smiled, sauntered over to the bookcase, and tugged the edge of it. "Right this way," she murmured.

What in the world was going on?

Drew's eyes were still sparkling when he took my

elbow and led me toward the hidden doorway.

What if I was walking into my death? What if Drew was a part of this? What if he was the man who'd broken into my home?

I stopped.

Drew leaned toward me and whispered, "Trust me."

I wanted to say, *Trust you? I don't even know you. Do you know how many people have wanted to kill me in my lifetime? In fact, there's a threat on my life right now.*

But, before I could, the sound of big band music drifted outward, as did the scent of food. What in the world . . . ?

Despite all my reservations, I followed the woman in black through the door. When I reached the other side, I sucked in a breath.

It was a restaurant.

Roaring-twenties-style decorations graced the place—deep burgundy wallpaper with chandeliers and thick tables. There were no windows, which made everything appear dark and intimate. People dined here, being waited on by women wearing flapper outfits and men dressed in vests and bow ties.

"What do you think?" Drew whispered.

"This is . . . a speakeasy?"

Satisfaction lit his gaze. "That's right. You have to give a password to get in. 'Punch the bag' actually was slang for small talk in the twenties."

I shook my head as I soaked everything in. This was amazing. Simply amazing. "I love it."

"I thought you might. Come on. I've got a table reserved in the corner."

A corner table? Could this evening get any better? I didn't think so.

***

Dinner ended. The braised chicken thighs I'd ordered were delicious, and the roasted asparagus had just the right crunch factor. Drew had ordered brisket with mashed potatoes. Apparently, he worked out, so he could afford the high calories.

The two of us had a great conversation, and I was again amazed at everything we had in common. Plus, Drew was such a gentleman. He'd helped me with my chair and coat. He'd opened doors and offered his arm.

He loved jazz music; he valued volunteer work; and he was active at church.

If I went down the list I'd made of one hundred qualities I wanted in a husband—sadly, yes, I had one of those—he'd fit almost all of them. I'd lost the list until recently, when I moved out of the house. I'd found it tucked into the pages of one of my old Bibles.

I was enjoying myself so much that I'd nearly forgotten about the danger plaguing me in recent days. This distraction had been nice.

"Do you know the detective who's on this case? Forgive me for being nosy. That was just the impression I was left with at the police station on Saturday."

My cheeks heated. How much did I say? There was no reason to skirt around the truth. "I . . . we . . . we used to date."

He nodded stiffly. "I see. Well, I hope I didn't bring

up a sour subject."

"No, you didn't. We're still friends."

"That's good. That says a lot about a relationship if you can remain friends."

I offered a quick smile. Breakup etiquette also dictated that it *wasn't* a good thing to remain friends. I supposed it depended on which expert you asked. "I think so also."

The waitress came over. "Same check or separate?"

"Separate, please," Drew said.

I blinked back my disappointment. Really? He'd been such a gentleman all evening and now we were splitting the check? I mean, I wasn't opposed to paying for myself but . . .

Drew nudged me, pulling me out of my stupor. "Just kidding. One check."

I released my breath with an airy laugh.

"I had you going for a minute," Drew said.

I wanted to deny it, but I couldn't. "You did."

"You were making a mental note to never go on any more dates with me."

"I didn't say that," I argued. My thoughts hadn't gone that far. But, eventually, they would have.

He chuckled. "I'm sorry to give you a hard time. I just couldn't resist."

I shrugged, feeling more at ease at his good-natured teasing.

He paid and, as we stepped outside, I realized it had started raining. With no windows inside the restaurant, I'd had no clue. And it was coming down in buckets, at that.

We paused under the awning. Neither of us had an umbrella.

"You know, in the old days, it would be customary for the man to lay down his coat over a puddle so a woman could cross without ruining her shoes," Drew started.

"Just think about all those jackets that were ruined," I said.

"Exactly! Certainly there was a more efficient way of doing things."

"I agree. I like to be treated like a lady, but that rule even makes me shrug. I have no idea what people were thinking." I nodded toward a particularly large puddle. "However, maybe you could bring a little stepping stone to put right there?"

"I have a better idea."

Before I could argue, he swept me into his arms. I sucked in a deep breath at his sudden move. With a grin, he carried me over the puddle before gently placing me back on my feet.

My heart raced out of control.

"How's that?" he asked.

I cleared my throat, trying to regain control of my thoughts. "Very efficient."

He shrugged and straightened his coat dramatically. "I like being efficient."

"You're good at it."

Raindrops hit my face and hair as I turned toward him. Our gazes caught.

If I weren't so skittish, this would be a perfectly romantic, kissable moment. I could see the desire in

Drew's eyes. I could feel our draw to each other.

But I wasn't ready. Kissing wasn't a big deal for a lot of people, but it was a big deal for me.

Drew winked and took my hand. "Come on."

As we hurried down the street, I heard a footfall behind us. My entire body went rigid.

I turned around, looking for the source of the sound and hoping desperately it was nothing.

The sidewalk behind us was empty.

"What's wrong?" Drew asked.

I tried to shrug off my apprehension. "Nothing, I guess."

But as we took a few more steps, I heard the sound again.

I glanced over my shoulder. A few people were leaving another restaurant, scrambling through the rain.

"Holly?" Drew asked.

"I think I'm hearing things," I confessed.

"Here's the parking garage," he said. "At least we can get you out of the rain."

My throat went dry. Parking garages didn't make me feel better. There were too many places for people to hide. It was too secluded, too dark, too everything.

I shivered when I stepped into the space, partly because of the rain and partly from fear.

As Drew started to lead me toward the elevator, I stopped. "Could we take the stairs?"

The request may have sounded unusual, but I felt safer on the stairs than I did trapped in an elevator.

"Sure thing. If that's what you want. Are you sure you're okay?"

I swallowed hard and ventured into the truth. "My intuition is telling me something is wrong. That someone's following us. The best thing we can do right now is to get out of here."

I thought he might react with disbelief. Instead, his jaw locked and he took my arm. "Let's get to our cars then."

As we hurried up the steps, I could hardly breathe. I waited for another footfall, another telltale sound.

I heard nothing.

As soon as we stepped onto the third level, my gaze darted from car to car. Someone could easily be waiting between any of them. My skin crawled as I anticipated someone emerging, jumping out, trying to end my life.

Drew kept a hand at my waist and pulled me close. He also appeared to be on edge, and his gaze darted around to all of the dark spaces and nooks here in the garage.

Finally, we reached our cars.

We'd made it.

But I knew I wasn't losing my mind. Someone had been out there.

"Do you want me to follow you home?" Drew asked.

I considered it a moment before shaking my head. I still wasn't sure I wanted him to know where I lived. "I'll be okay. Thank you."

"Are you sure?"

I nodded.

He still hesitated but finally nodded. "If you insist. I'll talk to you later then."

He glanced into the backseat, as if checking it for me,

before climbing into his own car.

My heart was still pounding out of control as I drove toward home.

Drew seemed too good to be true. But was he? Or did guys like him really exist?

I mean, he'd talked about the importance of family over career. He wanted children. A lot of them. He even had a retirement account set up. He'd paid off his student loans, and I was pretty sure he'd never even gone through a rebellious streak. That said a lot.

In fact, he kind of sounded like me.

But the question still lingered in the back of my head. Could he be involved with this mystery? Or were all my suspicions getting the best of me?

CHAPTER 16

When I got back home, Blake was inside, sitting on my couch with a computer on her lap. Her shoes were strewn by the door, a sweater had been tossed over the entryway table, and some socks were balled on the floor in front of her.

I resisted the urge to pick up after her, while inwardly twitching at the messes scattered over my house. If she stayed much longer I'd need to have a talk with her about it, but right now she was in the grace-filled honeymoon period of being my guest.

"I see you figured out the security system okay." I dropped my purse on the table beside the door, mentally making a note to put it in my room later, and took my sweater off.

"Yes, I did. I didn't set off any alarms. That's always a good thing."

"I'd say."

Blake closed her computer.

I wanted to greet her warmly and without hesitation. But everything my brother and sister—as well as Jamie and Chase—had said slammed into my head.

Had Alex and Ralph gotten their background checks back yet? If so, what had they discovered? And why couldn't I do something nice without all these reservations?

Blake gave an approving nod. "Don't you look nice. You have a very romantic, Jane Austin vibe going on. What's the occasion?"

"I had a date." I sucked in a long breath, inhaling the scent of a recently heated microwave dinner, which twisted my stomach. I wasn't a fan of processed foods. At all.

Blake's eyes lit. "Really? Sounds interesting. This non-dating gal would love to live vicariously through you."

"I don't know if there's anything worthy of living through me. He's a really nice guy, though." I sat across from her and tucked the skirt of my dress beneath my legs.

"What about that detective guy? Do you know him? You seemed to be pretty cozy when you talked."

I swallowed hard. "We were engaged."

Her eyes widened. "Really? Wow. He's . . . he's hot. Does that mean . . . does that mean he's back on the market since you're dating someone else?"

Something territorial started to rise in me. I wanted to scream no! But the truth was, Chase was officially a free man.

"Let's talk about you," I said, changing the subject. "How are you today?"

"I've been busy with school. I can't stop thinking

about what happened last night, though." She frowned as if apprehensive. "Have you heard any updates?"

I shook my head. "Unfortunately, I haven't. The intruder seemed pretty slick. He didn't leave any evidence behind."

"That's scary stuff."

"I know."

Her eyes brightened. "Oh, and someone stopped by a few hours ago. They said they were your future in-laws?"

My stomach sank. The Hookers. How had they gotten my address? "Did they say anything else?"

"They asked if you could stop by the funeral home tomorrow and help plan someone's memorial service."

Of course, Travis would have a memorial service. It was probably going to be at Wilford, for that matter.

"They also said they didn't have your phone number. That's why they came here."

"Good to know. Thanks for passing that on."

She shifted, and I noticed her thick gold bracelet. She also wore a coordinating necklace with a diamond pendant on the end.

"Nice set of jewelry," I said.

She looked down and her cheeks flushed. "Oh, these. My parents handed them down to me from my grandmother. They're kind of special to me."

"That's nice."

She let out a long breath and relaxed her shoulders, signaling a conversation change. "In case I haven't told you, I really appreciate you letting me stay here. I'm looking for somewhere else, but it's complicated being on a student income. Which basically means having no income."

"I remember what that was like."

I settled back on the couch, and Blake talked about classes and the weather and a new club she wanted to check out. As she talked, I only had one thought circling in my head.

What could two guys who moved dead bodies for a living be up to? That was the question.

***

Somewhere in the midst of trying to sleep and not being able to because of haunting memories of last night's break-in, a realization hit me like lightning.

What would two guys who moved dead bodies for a living be up to? That had been the question I was thinking about as I tried to drift to sleep.

But I'd also been thinking about Blake's jewelry and how hand-me-downs like that were so important to some people.

That's when it hit me that Travis and Chuck were both in the perfect position to take people's valuables.

After all, they were often in a room alone as they prepared to take away a deceased loved one.

Dr. Gilbert had said that Travis was looking through his wife's lingerie drawer. But what if he was really looking for valuables? What if he wasn't a perv at all?

That could also explain how he'd come into money recently.

If Travis and Chuck were working with someone,

that third person might be desperate to keep what they were doing quiet. To save his reputation? Possibly. Or maybe it was so he could keep profiting from it.

Maybe Travis and Chuck had decided they wanted out. Wasn't that what Travis had told Ronald? That he was going to turn things around? Maybe in the process they were going to bring down the third partner. Maybe they'd saved evidence against him, evidence that someone now thought I had.

Maybe it was a stretch, but it was the best I had to work with right now.

Unable to sleep, I hopped on my computer. I logged into the crime reports for the city. I looked through anything that had to do with stolen jewelry.

People's names weren't mentioned, but their addresses were. I printed them out and sat back to study them.

I eliminated many of them, starting with those from other areas of town. Most people who used Dillow's service were probably in this area. Not necessarily all of them, but in my experience people liked to stick close to home with stuff like this.

I also narrowed it down to the last three months, just to simplify things.

Then I looked at the addresses.

One stood out to me. I recognized that street and house number.

One of my former social-work clients lived there.

I knew what I was doing. First thing tomorrow morning, I was going to call her and see if I could find out more information.

And, for now, I would keep this quiet from Chase. Right now, all this was just a theory. I needed to find out more information before I brought the case before him.

***

I was sitting at my desk at work the next day when a woman came to see me. She was in her mid-thirties with dark hair pulled back into a sloppy ponytail. Tendrils escaped, but not in a flattering way. More in a haired-out manner. Deep bags formed half-circles beneath her eyes, and her blue shirt had a stain on the chest.

It took me a minute to recognize her before memories flooded back to me. This was Rita Chaplin. She was a single mom who'd had her kids taken away for six months while she got herself clean. I'd been right there in the thick of things as a social worker.

Eventually Rita had straightened up, found a job, and moved in with her mom to help her pay bills. I'd followed up with her in the months after to make sure the kids were safe. Through that, we'd developed somewhat of a professional friendship.

"Holly," she started.

"Rita." I rose and pulled her into a hug. "It's been a long time."

She fidgeted nervously, apprehension shooting from her like solar waves. "It has been."

I patted the seat near my desk. "Thanks for coming."

Her bloodshot eyes met mine. "I'm glad you reached out. No one else has seemed to care."

"Do you want some coffee? Something to eat?"

"No, I'm fine. Thank you, though."

I leaned on my elbows toward her. "I know you were probably surprised when I called you. I just happened to see your address when I was going through some crime reports. Someone broke in and stole some jewelry?"

She swallowed hard and lowered her eyes. "That's right."

"Can you tell me what happened?"

"It was my mom's. She passed away three weeks ago."

I reached forward and squeezed her arm. When I saw the tears glistening in her eyes, I handed her a tissue, and she fisted it in her hands.

"Oh, Rita, I'm so sorry," I murmured. "I know the two of you were close."

She nodded, her chin trembling and her hand still clutching the Kleenex. "I miss her terribly."

"I'm sure you do. She was a wonderful person." And she had been. Their relationship had been estranged when Rita was deep into the drug culture. But her mom had been waiting for her with open arms the moment Rita decided to walk away from that life. "How are the kids handling it?"

Rita shrugged and wiped beneath her eyes. "As well as can be expected."

I waited for her to gather her thoughts—perhaps her courage.

Finally, her weary gaze fluttered up to mine. "Last week I went into a local pawnshop to look for an iPad for my teenager. I was hoping I could find one for cheap."

"Smart thinking."

"As I was there, I couldn't help but look at the jewelry. It's always a temptation to buy something for myself, but I never do. I just don't have the money." She paused for long enough to draw in a deep breath. "Anyway, I saw this bracelet. It was beautiful and gold with jade stones on each of the links. My mom had one just like it. In fact, she wanted to be buried with it."

A feeling of dread dropped into my stomach. I thought I knew where she was going with this, but I really hoped I didn't. "Is that right?"

She nodded. "So, of course, I wanted to see it, just for the memory if nothing else. It reminded me so much of my mom. I nearly burst into tears right there in the shop. The man took the bracelet out of the case and let me see it. As I turned it over, I saw an inscription on the back."

I held my breath, waiting for her to finish.

Please let me be wrong, Lord. Please.

"You can imagine my surprise when I saw my mother's initials there, along with the date it was given to her by my father."

I closed my eyes, wishing what she'd told me wasn't true. "Oh, Rita. I'm so sorry."

"Me too. I just had no idea. I wasn't expecting it."

I waited until two coworkers walked past before responding quietly with, "You obviously reported it."

Her face twisted in a frown. Not a pouty frown, but a frown that came from somewhere deep inside her soul. "I did. But you know how I feel about the police. They may be good guys, but I've had one too many run-ins with them. As soon as they see my rap sheet, they don't take me seriously."

I'd heard this story one too many times. Too many people in the inner city viewed the cops as enemies. It was a shame on so many different levels.

"I understand," I whispered. "But I'm glad you reported it. Did they follow up?"

She shook her head. "Not that I can tell. They didn't seem that interested."

And that was also a shame on so many levels. "Did you talk to the pawnshop owner to see if you could get information from him, at least?"

"He said it came in last week, and that it was from one of his reputable sellers." She frowned as she remembered the conversation.

"Did he give you a name?"

Rita shook her head, tears threatening to overflow from her eyelids down her cheeks. "No, he refused. He didn't seem to take me very seriously either. I'm not naïve. I know people think I have no power. I look poor. I don't speak proper English. Anyone would know I don't have money to fight any legal battles. I don't even have a good reputation."

My heart panged with compassion toward her at the helplessness in her words. My phone began ringing. I didn't recognize the number, so I let it go, not wanting to interrupt this conversation.

Her weary eyes met mine. "Do you think you can help me? I know this isn't a big deal for most people. But it's a big deal to me. Someone shouldn't be getting away with this."

"I'm definitely going to look into this."

"I've heard about your reputation." Her voice lost some of its gentleness. "I only know you through your social work, but I know that you've helped people in the past. Helped people like me."

Her words inspired me. She was right. I was passionate about helping others, whether it was through anonymous financial donations or cleaning their houses or helping them put their questions to rest.

"I'll be happy to do whatever I can," I said.

"Oh, thank you." She reached toward me and gave me another hug. The scent of cigarette smoke and cheap shampoo filled my nostrils.

I leaned back, tapping my fingers on the desk as I pondered the situation. "When was the last time you saw this jewelry?"

"It was in her room when she died. It was her favorite bracelet. The piece wasn't extremely valuable, but she loved it."

"Who had access to the room after she died?"

She shook her head. "Me and my kids mostly. We didn't host anything at our house. Instead, we went to my aunt's place."

"That makes it hard to know how someone would get it. Were there any break-ins recently?"

"No, there weren't. But I do have one theory. You're going to think I'm crazy."

"Please, tell me. You're not crazy."

"On the night my mom died, we had this company transport her body. One of the workers was acting really funny. I had a bad feeling about him."

I closed my eyes as the truth hit me. "What was the name of the company?"

"I'm not sure. I called the funeral home, and they're the ones that set everything up."

I nodded, understanding the injustice of it. She didn't have to convince me. "What funeral home did you use, Rita?"

Her bloodshot gaze met mine. "That one over on Eighth Street."

All the fluid drained from my face. "You mean Wilford?"

She nodded. "That's the one."

CHAPTER 17

I leaned back in my seat and sighed. I'd escaped to my car during lunch break. It was the only place I felt like I could find my sanity for a moment. I needed quiet to digest all that I'd learned and to figure out my next step.

Perry Como crooned from my speakers, encouraging me to catch a falling star and put it in my pocket. Yes, I'd been on a Perry kick lately, and I made no apologies about it.

I'd promised Rita before she'd left that I would try and get to the bottom of what had happened. But that meant I'd be entering some murky waters in the meantime. I'd been there before. But I also had to keep in mind that I'd almost gotten killed before in the process.

I knew one thing: there was a good chance I'd stumbled upon some answers. I just needed to verify a few more things before I told Chase. I needed to know why Travis had targeted me. He'd picked me as his date on purpose. I also needed to know why Chuck had whispered, "Be careful."

To think that all of that was planned with some

ulterior motives didn't bring me any comfort.

Just then, my phone rang. I glanced at the screen and saw it was Alex. I knew exactly what she was calling about. As I grabbed my phone, I noted the dried grass stuck in my carpet and made a mental note to clean the car this weekend.

"Hey, sis," I said. "What's going on?"

"I just got the criminal background check back on Blake," she started. "I thought you'd want to know she's clean."

"That's good news." Despite that, my sister still sounded uncertain.

"Blake Hallowell does appear to be her real name. The bad news is that we can't look into the details of the adoption. It was closed, so I have no way of verifying that story without a lot more digging."

"Also good to know." Momentary relief washed through me. At least one person in my life had checked out. I wasn't sure about the rest of the people who'd come into my life recently.

"That still doesn't mean we can trust her." Alex's voice was firm, leaving no room for question or doubt. "I still find it strange that she'd want to connect with us."

That was Alex. She saw things in black and white, and she was very slow to change her mind once she made it up.

"People like to have a sense of family," I argued. I would have done the same thing in Blake's shoes. Maybe that's why I felt such a connection to her.

"That's the thing. She has a lot of family. I really don't know why she feels the need to find more."

"It seems like human nature to me. Most people are naturally curious." Except Alex. Well, she was curious, but only when it came to professional development. It was never just because.

"Maybe you're right." It had probably pained her to say that. "But I suggest we tread with caution until we know more."

A splash of irritation hit me. I just wanted life to be simple, but life never seemed to be simple when there was more than one person involved. "We won't know more about Blake until we get to know her."

"That's true. But we should *cautiously* get to know her."

I was about to argue again, when Alex continued.

"Do you want to see if she'd like to meet with all of us? Maybe for dinner this weekend?"

Well, that was a surprise. Shocking, actually. "Sure, I'm sure I can arrange that."

"Sounds good. I'll let Ralph know. And don't talk to her again without us."

Should I tell her the truth? That Blake was staying with me? I decided not to. I was a big girl. I could make my own choices, whether my brother and sister liked it or not.

And I really, really hoped I didn't have to eat crow and admit at any point that I was wrong.

Before I went back inside, my phone buzzed.

It was another text from Travis's phone.

I held my breath as I read the words there.

Still being nosy? You're wearing on my patience. Back off. Last warning. Next time

I follow you I won't be so polite.

***

After work, I picked Jamie up from her house, and we headed to the pawnshop where Rita had found her mother's bracelet.

Jamie was always up for coming along for the ride, especially if there might be trouble. She'd just been promoted to crime reporter for a local community newspaper. I supposed this would give her insight into what was going on, and she could later spin it for her column. Win-win, right?

As we drove there, I gave her an update on everything I'd learned today, ending with the latest text I'd received—and, of course, I'd reported it all to Chase, as promised.

"You've been busy," she said, slipping on some oversized sunglasses that made her look oh so glamorous.

"Tell me about it." I gripped the steering wheel, my conversation with Alex still echoing in my head. I didn't want to be bothered by it. I really didn't, but I was. Now I had to figure out what to do about it.

Jamie settled back against the seat as the city streets blurred past. "I will say that life is never boring around you, Holly Anna."

"I'm not sure if I should apologize or say thanks."

"Me neither." She made a face.

I made a face back.

"And get this. I emailed Luke."

I snapped my head toward her. "Luke who ditched us on the night of the murder?"

"The one and only. I asked him where he went. I may have said some other not so nice things."

"And?"

"He apologized," Jamie said. "Said he ran into an old friend, and they started catching up. At that point, we were already talking to the police, and he figured our date was doomed. His words, not mine."

"He still should have come back. It's common decency."

"I agree. He was a loser."

I stole another glance at my friend, trying to read her expression. "So, are you going to continue your online dating spree?"

She shrugged, an aloof air about her. "I haven't decided yet. There is one other thing."

"What's that?"

"Wesley is back in town."

I gripped the wheel, really not expecting that news. "Is he? Have you talked?"

Jamie had liked him. She'd liked him a lot. I had also. I thought the two of them were good together.

"He wants to meet this weekend," Jamie said.

I sucked in a breath, knowing the emotional turmoil this could cause my friend. "And?"

She shrugged. "I'm thinking about it."

"Why wouldn't you?"

Even with her sunglasses on, I could sense her mood darkening. "Because he didn't think I was worth waiting around for, that's why."

I heard an edge of hurt in her voice. "You think he was hoping to meet someone else on this cross-country bicycling trip?"

She offered a terse shrug. "Maybe he wanted to keep his options open."

"Or maybe he really was just trying to be fair to you."

"Maybe." She sounded unconvinced.

I glanced back at the road in front of me, trying to remember where I was supposed to turn. "Well, I think you should meet with him."

"And I think you should go out with Drew again."

My bottom lip dropped open at her subject change. "Oh, and I see what you're doing. You're turning the tables on me."

"Of course. I'm deflecting. But it's a good kind of deflecting. The kind that takes the attention from me."

I thought it through, honestly surprised by her words. I'd always thought she liked Chase. "Don't you feel like you're betraying Chase by saying that? I mean, you liked him too. I thought you thought we were perfect together."

She released a long breath. "I don't know. I mean, I did like him. I mean, I *do* like him. But that relationship has a dead-end sign at the end of the road. I would have broken up with him also if I were in your shoes. Your goals for the future don't align, and that's a serious problem."

"He's had a difficult life." Why was I defending him? "I mean, his mom left when he was six. His dad raised him—if that's what you'd want to call it. And then Chase found out he had a brother because his dad was a cheater. One year after meeting him face-to-face, his brother is murdered."

"I'm not saying he hasn't had it tough. And I know you want to be there for him. But you don't have to date to be there for him. I'd like to see you look out for yourself every once in a while, instead of trying to fix everyone else."

I pulled into the pawnshop parking lot just in time to freeze—car and all. "What do you mean?"

I stared at Jamie, wanting to see her response so I could measure her sincerity and the truth in her words.

Jamie practically snorted, not the least bit affected by her jarring words. "Don't tell me you don't know that's what you do. You're drawn to broken people. You want to help them, to make their lives better. It's like your mission in life. But that's not what a forever relationship should be built on. That's why I like Drew. He has his act together."

I wasn't quite ready to agree with her. "Or so it seems. I mean, two of his associates were murdered."

"He probably had nothing to do with that."

"Probably being the keyword here." Or did he? Another sense of dread shot through me.

I remembered what Ronald had said about Drew valuing his reputation. Would he be willing to go as far as murder to protect his good name?

I really didn't think so. But I'd be a fool not to consider every fact.

"Okay, Ms. Crime Reporter." I reactivated my body and finished pulling into a parking space. "Let's do some more digging."

***

"I don't know what you're talking about," the pawnshop owner said.

He practically pretended we weren't there or weren't worth his time. He continued to check some inventory against a list in his hands, barely making eye contact with us.

"There was a bracelet with jade stones here earlier this week," I explained, irritation growing in me. I leaned on the glass display case, my fingers leaving their prints over the very glass he'd been cleaning as we walked in. "Did you sell it?"

The man, a gruff-looking male with frizzy white-blond hair and a scraggily mustache, paused for long enough to give me a death stare. He wore a stained T-shirt, had yellow teeth, and his eyelids drooped.

His expression was all business as he deadpanned, "Yep. Sorry."

Irritation continued to rise like lava in an erupting volcano. Didn't this man know about the importance of eye contact during conversations? "Who brought the jewelry in?"

"I'm not at liberty to discuss that." He placed a check mark in one of his columns. "Privacy and all."

"Did this person bring anything else in?" Jamie asked. "Any other jewelry?"

"I can't say that either."

I turned to my friend, deciding to try a different approach. Now I just hoped that Jamie would play along.

"Even if they did, the police would have taken that also, right? You've done stories about instances like these before."

She nodded. "Most likely. I'll include that nugget in my crime report."

The man lowered his notebook, his attention suddenly on us. "Whoa, whoa, whoa. What crime report?"

Jamie's hand went to her hip. "I'm with the newspaper. I do a column on crime in the area. Stolen goods ending up at a pawnshop? I know it's nothing unusual, but with the funeral home twist, I'm sure readers will find it very eye-opening. Especially when they find out that you're involved with it."

The man narrowed his snake-like eyes. "I ain't involved with anything."

"You're protecting someone," I said.

"If I have issues, I take them up with the police. Not with prissy little girls."

Fire ignited through me, but before I could retort, Jamie did. "Can you answer this: has this person brought in items before?"

"It's a possibility."

Well, that was something. Not much but I'd take whatever I could get. "How many more items?"

"Quite a few, truth be told. I didn't know they were stolen. And not stolen from dead people, at that."

"When did you find out that fact?" I asked.

"When that lady came in, claiming it was her mom's bracelet. I didn't think she was telling the truth. But I do know thieves try to use places of business such as mine to sell their loot. I don't want anything to do with those kinds of people."

I thought he was telling the truth. There was something about the set of his shoulders, his chin, that told me he had a lot of pride. He might be rude, and his store might be dirty, but the man thought of himself as a wise businessman.

Once we were back in my car, Jamie and I debriefed. "So, if I'm reading this situation correctly, all this centers around a crime theft ring that steals jewelry from the homes of dead people," I said.

Jamie nodded slowly, still staring straight ahead at the pawnshop. "Aren't there easier ways to earn money?"

"They can probably justify this. I mean, after all, this jewelry no longer belongs to anyone. Kind of. They probably think they aren't hurting anyone since the owner is already dead."

"That's despicable."

"It really is," I said. "If this theory is true, then the body movers are behind it."

"One would think. The other thing I don't understand is that there doesn't seem to be a lot of money involved. I mean, maybe they're making a thousand or so dollars. Is it really worth it to go through all this trouble just for that amount? Is it worth it to murder someone?"

"Good questions. Maybe the person behind this is a family member of someone Travis and Chuck stole from. Maybe this person felt like Travis and Chuck were capitalizing on their loss. Maybe his anger was compounded with his grief and led him to be irrational—to a deadly extent."

"It's a possibility. But it does seem extreme."

"Any time there's a murder, that's extreme," Jamie said.

"I can't argue with that." I kept thinking. "What if there's someone else involved with this theft ring?"

"Well, if there is a third person, then maybe the person in charge of coordinating these thefts is the one behind the murders. Maybe he wants more money for himself. Or the other guys were getting sloppy, and he was afraid they'd be caught."

I leaned back into my seat, wishing I could make sense of things. But I needed more information first.

"At least, it's a start," I finally said. "It's better than the nothing we had to go on before."

"But where do we go now?" Jamie asked.

I let out a long breath. "That's an excellent question. How would we find out who the ringleader is? I'm inclined to think it's someone they worked with."

"We're getting closer by the minute. I can feel it."

I agree. But, unfortunately, the faces that drifted through my mind as potential suspects were unnerving.

Ronald. Raul. Even Drew.

***

Despite my reservations, I decided to head to the funeral home so I could meet with the Hookers about the memorial service. I got there early in hopes of talking to Drew first.

I'd already called Chase and told him what I'd discovered. I figured I had enough information that it would warrant looking into, and Chase had agreed. He was going to see what he could find out.

There were only a few cars in the parking lot when I pulled in, Drew's Mustang among them. The confirmation that he was here caused a rush of nerves to sweep through me. Uncomfortable conversations had never been my favorite thing. Not by a long shot.

Nor had I ever really liked funeral homes. They brought back too many sad memories. Mostly they brought back memories of being there after my dad died. Those were some of the hardest days of my life.

As soon as I stepped onto the plush burgundy carpet of the foyer, those memories rushed back with a vengeance. Grief hadn't been as constant a companion lately, but it was still there, showing up like an unwelcome guest and lingering for as long as it pleased. Its presence showed that I'd loved and I'd loved well, but its absence helped me to look to the future instead of the past.

"Can I help you?" A woman appeared from an office in the distance. Recognition spread across her face. "We met. At the get-together for Travis."

"Alicia, right?"

She nodded. "That's right. And you are . . ."

"Holly."

"Good to see you again, Holly. How can I help you?"

I wiped my damp hands on my floral-print dress. "I'm here to see Drew."

"Do you have an appointment?" She fluttered her

long eyelashes politely and patiently as she waited.

I shook my head, remaining somber. Was there any other way to act at a funeral home? "No, I don't. If it's a bad time, I can come later."

"Let me see—"

Before she could step away, Drew emerged from one of the doorways in the distance. A wide grin spread across his face when he spotted me, and, for a moment, my nerves dissipated.

"I thought I recognized that voice." He crossed the room until he reached me. "This is a nice surprise."

He took my arm and led me into his office, where he shut the door. I settled onto the couch there. Drew sat on the other end, but still close enough that our knees slightly touched.

I stared at his warm, brown eyes a moment. I couldn't believe I was here or that I was doing this. Those eyes beckoned trust, and Drew had been nothing but kind to me since we'd met.

That was the very reason I had to come to him with what I knew. It was the right thing. A lot of times the hard thing and the right thing went hand in hand.

"It's good to see you," he started.

"I'm sorry to stop by unannounced." I glanced around his office, suddenly curious about his career. "Tell me about your job here."

He leaned back. "It's truly a family business, even though I'm the CEO. My mom is a funeral director. My dad oversees cremation. My sister and her husband do a little bit of everything, but mainly act as funeral attendants."

"I had no idea you had such a large staff."

"It's surprising how many people are needed to make sure things run smoothly."

"I thought you had a brother also," I said. "Didn't I see you with him at the memorial lunch?"

His gaze darkened. "I do. Raul. He doesn't want much to do with the business, although he will fill in on occasion. This line of work just isn't his cup of tea. Nor is anything that requires empathy."

"Ouch."

Drew shook his head. "Sorry. I shouldn't have said that. He's been a bit of a thorn in my side lately."

"It sounds like you guys are opposites."

"In every way."

I could tell he didn't want to talk about this anymore. I decided to give the conversation a break.

"So, are you hands-on or are you the businessman here?"

"A little of both. I do the embalmings, usually. I meet with the family and explain their options. I review the forms for bone and tissue donation—"

"You do that here? I thought it was done in the hospital."

"Organ donation is. I work with a local company, Life Force, to secure the bone and tissue. There's quite a bit of paperwork, however, that needs to be filled out first. It can be time-consuming. My brother, Raul, was actually a recipient of a tissue donation."

"Really? May I ask why?"

"He has some heart problems," Drew explained. "He needed to have a valve replaced, and they were able to secure what was needed from a tissue donor."

"That's pretty amazing."

He shifted his weight. "I don't suppose you came in expecting to hear all of that."

"No, it's all very interesting, though." I pressed my lips together, this conversation feeling like a weight around my neck that wanted to strangle my words before they could escape. "I wish I was here just to be social."

He flinched ever-so-slightly. "I wish that was the reason you were here as well. What's going on, Holly? I can tell something is bothering you."

I drew in a deep breath before starting. "Two things. The Hookers asked me to come and help them plan the memorial service."

His eyes widened. "That sounds awkward."

"I'm going to have to tell them the truth, but I keep avoiding it. So here I am. But I got here early to talk to you."

"Okay."

I handed him the paper with the addresses on it. "Is there any way you could cross-reference these addresses with clients who have used your services here?"

He stared at the paper. "I . . . I suppose I could. It would be tedious but possible. What's going on?"

"I know this is going to sound crazy, but I talked to a woman today whom I met a few years ago through my job as a social worker. Her mother recently passed away, and she used Wilford for the arrangements."

"Okay." He straightened his sleeves, his intense gaze

never leaving mine. But there was also a softness there, a compassionate undertone.

Keep going, Holly. You're not done yet. "She found a piece of her mother's jewelry at a pawnshop recently. The last time anyone saw it was in her mother's room when she died. Her mom was supposed to be buried with it."

I held my breath, waiting with dread for his reaction. But I hadn't spelled everything out yet. There was still more to be said.

Drew's eyes widened, but his voice remained soft. "What are you saying, Holly?"

"She believes someone took the bracelet and sold it to the pawnshop to make some extra cash."

"Who is she looking at? Family? A lot of people are in and out during those final moments."

I rubbed my lips together. "She believes it was one of the death transportation response—" What were they called again? My mind went blank. "Deceased haulage specialists?"

Drew's eyes sparkled. "Just call them what everyone else does: body movers."

"Got it."

The sparkle in his gaze disappeared. "Holly, I have a hard time believing that anyone I hired would ever do that."

I paused, trying to choose my words kindly so this didn't turn into a turbulent conversation. "Then how did it happen?"

"Are you sure this woman is telling you the truth? You know how people are litigation happy nowadays.

Maybe this is one of those cases, like the people who plant dead mice in their soda cans and then tell the world the bottling company put it there."

Again, I paused. "I can see where you'd want to question that. But I don't believe she's lying. And, if what you're saying is true, she would have gone to a lawyer or maybe even to the media. She talked to me instead."

"Why did she do that?"

"Because there are only a few people she trusts around here. I'm one of them."

He leaned back and pressed his lips together. "I can't stomach the thought of someone I know doing this."

"Do you have any other ideas on how this could have happened?"

He hung his head, swung it back and forth, keeping a hand across his forehead. I let him have his moment to process this.

"She's certain no one in her family did this?"

I nodded. "She said there were very few people in and out."

"I see." He let out a long sigh. "Would you give me her name?"

"Rita Chaplin."

He crossed the room and reached his computer. He typed in a few things before leaning back with a grunt.

"What is it?"

"Travis was one of the people who picked up her mother."

I closed my eyes. "That's what I was afraid of."

"What about these other addresses?" He studied the

paper with a frown.

"They're other people in this area who reported jewelry thefts in the past three months."

"And you think . . ." His voice faded. He knew exactly what I was getting at. "I'll see what I can find out."

"If you could keep it just between us for now. There's someone else involved with this, Drew, and we don't know who that is yet."

"I understand."

I considered myself a pretty good reader of people, and I felt certain that Drew was telling the truth. "I'm sorry, Drew."

"No, I'm glad you came to me. Thank you. I suppose this makes more sense now. Maybe Travis and Chuck were in some kind of business together, stealing jewelry from the deceased. It's despicable."

"It is."

"Have you told the police yet?"

I nodded. "I did. I realize it has the potential to make your business look bad, and I apologize for that."

"No, it was the right thing to do."

My stomach clenched. "There's one other thing. Remember that Travis and Chuck both ended up dead."

He blanched. "You think someone killed them over this?"

If only I knew that. "We don't know how deep this goes or what's really going on. Questioning people could put you in danger."

Just then, someone knocked at the door. When Drew opened the door, I saw AJ standing there. Only he looked different. He wore a suit and tie instead of his suspenders and bowtie.

"Hey there." Recognition flickered across his face. "We met before."

"That's right. At Travis's memorial lunch."

"That's right. Drew and I had a meeting. Do I need to reschedule?"

I stood, having no intentions of interrupting Drew's schedule. "I actually have an appointment."

As soon as I said the words, voices drifted into the office. The Hookers.

I was going to have to tell them the truth.

And I wasn't looking forward to it.

CHAPTER 18

"Is there anything here you see that you'd like to keep in Travis's memory?"

Mama Hooker stared at me as we stood in the living room of Travis's apartment.

As I feared, my talk with them hadn't gone well. Even though I'd told them Travis and I weren't together, they'd insisted that I'd been an important part of his life.

They'd also insisted that I still help with the memorial service, and then they'd asked if I wanted to go to Travis's place with them to go through a few things. I'd almost said no. I *should* have said no. But the nosy part of me found the word "sure" coming from my lips.

So here I was.

Travis's apartment was pretty unimpressive. Not only was it rundown, but I'd seen a cockroach when I'd walked up the stairwell. His neighbors yelled upstairs. The whole place smelled like trash that hadn't been taken out in weeks.

The inside was no better—mostly hand-me-down furniture from the eighties. Leftover food rested on the kitchen counter and on the dining room table and on the entertainment center. Piles of magazines and newspapers were stacked against one wall.

I glanced around, knowing that Mama Hooker was waiting for my response.

"I . . . uh . . . I don't know," I finally said.

"I'm surprised he doesn't have any pictures of you here." Mama Hooker frowned.

"How'd you get your hands on the ones you had at the lunch?" I'd been meaning to ask them that.

"He mailed them to us, of course."

"Of course." I walked toward the bookcase and picked up another picture of Travis with someone else. A guy. They both held fish in front of them, and the green background made me think they were camping. "Who's this?"

"Jason Lewis," Mama Hooker said. "Certainly you met him."

She must have forgotten that I hadn't really been dating Travis.

When I didn't say anything, she continued.

"They're best friends. Did everything together."

"He didn't come to the luncheon," I said.

"That's because he was in Wisconsin visiting his family. He came back Tuesday. We've already spent quite a bit of time with him. But then he had to go back to work at that appliance store downtown."

"Did he ever tell you about this table?" Papa Hooker knocked on a wooden coffee table.

"I can't say he did."

"I built this for him," he said. "He went through this James Bond phase and drew up the plans for this himself."

I stared at the boxy table. "Is there something James Bond-y about it?"

"Well, of course. Check this out." Papa Hooker reached beneath the ledge around the top. A moment later, a door popped open.

My eyes widened when I saw stacks and stacks of cash inside.

I knew one thing: there was no way Travis had gotten that money through small-time jewelry theft. Something else was going on here.

***

"So, Travis had a stash of money hidden in a secret compartment in his coffee table?" Jamie asked me that evening as we shared some gluten-free pizza.

I replayed the incident in my head. I wouldn't believe it either if I hadn't been there. "Ten thousand dollars."

"Where did he get that kind of money?"

"I have no idea, nor did his parents."

"And you called Chase?" Jamie asked.

"Of course. I had no choice."

"And after all that, the Hookers still consider you their almost daughter-in-law?"

I remembered their enamored expressions. They seemed to think I could do no harm. "Pretty much."

"That's . . . what can I say? These things would only happen to you." Jamie stared at me from across the table, a hint of amusement in her gaze and her slightly upturned lip.

I scowled. "I know."

"I've got to figure out how to get more answers," I said. "I feel like I'm stumbling through this. I want to get involved, yet I don't want to get involved."

"Any ideas on how to figure out those answers?" She took a long sip of her water and made a face. "Too much vinegar."

Yes, my friend was crazy, and she added apple cider vinegar to her water because it apparently had amazing health benefits. She'd convinced me to try it once, and I decided to stick with just lemons instead.

"The Hookers mentioned that Travis had a best friend named Jason and that he works at an appliance store downtown. I'd like to track him down."

"Seems like a good start."

"At least it's something." I frowned.

"What do you think is going on?" She took a bite of her pizza, cheese stringing from her mouth all the way to the plate as she put her slice back there.

"My first thought was jewelry. Now I think it's something bigger than that. There was too much cash there for them just to be stealing a necklace here or there."

"What else could it be?"

"I have no idea. I think when I figure out why Travis wanted to go on a date with me, I'll have some answers. It obviously wasn't for my vintage good looks. He targeted me." I shivered at the words.

"It's all strange."

"I really need to think a little harder about that key

also. Somehow it's connected also. The Texter keeps calling it 'information.' How in the world do I begin to figure out what lock that key fits into?"

"What's your guess?"

"Maybe it's a warehouse where they were stashing their loot?"

"Warehouse?" She quirked her eyebrow again. "That would be a lot of jewelry. Like, a lot."

"Storage unit?" I suggested.

"Seems like they'd be spending all their profit to rent a place like that."

"Safety deposit box?"

"Don't they usually have smaller keys than the one you found?"

"I'm not sure," I said. "I've never had one."

She sighed and leaned back, looking thoughtfully in the distance. "Maybe you can ask that Jason guy about it. Maybe it unlocks a desk or something."

"He's my only hope right now. I have nightmares about this guy coming back and demanding the 'information' from me."

"Didn't Chase arrest someone for this crime?" Jamie asked.

I nodded. "He did. Ronald, who owned the transportation company."

"So, he's either working with someone or Chase arrested the wrong person?"

I nodded again. "I think so."

"Well, we have lots of questions. We just need to find some answers."

"Without getting killed," I added.

She snorted. "Yeah, without getting killed first."

Just then, Chase texted me.

Ronald Dillow has been cleared. His alibi checked out. Just thought you'd want to know.

***

As I headed back to my house, I wondered if Blake would be there yet.

I had some conflicting emotions about seeing her. I wanted to believe her intentions were good and pure. But Alex's and Ralph's words kept ringing in my ears about how I shouldn't be too trusting.

Blake was sitting on my couch when I got back, her laptop on her legs and a textbook or two or three scattered beside her—again.

"Hey, Holly! You're back." She quickly began straightening her books.

"Don't worry about it." I sat down in a chair across from her. "How's it going?"

She shrugged. "I have a big project I'm working on. As soon as it's over, I'm going to look for a new place to live so I can get out of your hair."

I didn't want her to think she was in my hair. That just seemed so rude. "You're fine. I understand that you need to focus on your schoolwork right now."

"Thank you. I appreciate it."

I leaned back. "So, do you miss farm living? I know Cincinnati is quite the change from Hillsboro."

"I do miss it. But city life is fun also."

"So, I've always wondered: do you ever get tired of eating eggs?"

She stared at me a moment, a strange look in her eyes. "What?"

"You said your family owned a chicken farm."

Her mouth formed an O. "Of course. Sorry. I was still thinking about what I had for dinner. And, no, I never get tired of it. My mom fixes eggs every way imaginable."

"My dad used to always talk about tidbitting. He said that's what my mom was doing when she got herself involved in all her clubs." I smiled at the memory.

But Blake met my gaze with another blank stare.

Had she never heard about tidbitting before?

"It's that little dance that roosters do where they bob their head and pick up and drop food," I told her.

"Oh, tidbitting. Of course. I'm spacing out today. You'll have to excuse me. I think my brain is fried from all this studying."

"That happens sometimes." I needed to give her the benefit of the doubt. Yet questions were pushing their way to the surface, and I didn't know how much longer I was going to be able to ignore them.

She let out a sigh. "Speaking of that, maybe I should get to bed. I need to be fresh for my exams tomorrow."

"Of course."

"Good night, Holly."

"Good night." As I watched her depart down the hallway, suddenly I felt anxious to have my place back to myself again.

CHAPTER 19

I locked myself in my room that night.

Something was bugging me.

It was the fact that coincidences were rarely coincidences.

The fact that Blake had shown up, claiming to be related, one day after Travis died was almost too much for me to believe. That seemed suspicious. I didn't like suspicious things.

Plus, had she really forgotten what tidbitting was? I wanted to give her the benefit of the doubt, while finding the balance between being as wise as a serpent and as gentle as a dove.

In the safety of my room with my door locked, I hopped on my own computer. I did a search for Blake Hallowell. I should have done this much sooner.

Maybe I'd been looking for a connection with my father, wanting it so badly that I'd believed too easily Blake was whom she claimed to be. The fact that we looked similar had sealed the deal for me—but had that been premature?

More than one Blake Hallowell popped up. I scrolled

through various profiles until I found my Blake's picture. It simply listed Ohio as her home state.

I scrolled through her posts and pictures. Blake definitely appeared to have a wild streak. There were lots of pictures of her partying at clubs and drinking, all while wearing tight outfits and too much mascara.

Those pictures didn't surprise me, though. I'd expected Blake to have a wild side. I was one of the few people I knew who didn't have a wild side, which made me either an anomaly or extremely boring.

Even though she was from a small town and her parents were farmers, she could easily pass for farm girls gone wild. I'd say getting older had calmed her down, but some of her recent pictures were of her partying. As in, two months ago.

Out of curiosity, I clicked back further, hoping to catch some glimpses of her family or life back in Hillsboro, Ohio. I didn't see any of her on the farm, only of her with her friends.

I scrolled through several pictures from last year before stopping. At first, I'd thought she wasn't in these photos. But when I slowed my scroll, I realized Blake was in these photos. She just looked different.

No longer did she have nearly the exact same hairstyle as I did. No, in these photos her hair was blonde, cut to her chin, with brown lowlights near her neck. She looked like a totally different person.

An ice-cold feeling swelled in my gut.

Had she chosen my hairstyle for a reason? Did she want to look like me before we met?

My online date had ulterior motives, and he was

now dead.

A man was texting threats to me and had broken into my home.

And now an imposter might be living with me.

Could this get any worse?

***

This was no time to be passive. I could hear a mental clock ticking like a bomb, reminding me with every second that I had to find this killer before he found me . . . again.

That was why, before work the next morning, I swung by Ronald Dillow's office. I had no idea if he'd be there or not, but it was worth a shot.

His business was located in a building attached to a storage-unit office. On the other side was an alteration business. I had a feeling the rent here was cheap. Why else would someone choose this location?

The parking lot had been full, so I'd had to park in some sort of overflow lot toward the back of the storage-unit-lined streets.

I took a deep breath when I reached his office door and hoped this paid off. I gripped the handle and twisted it. The door stuck.

But it was unlocked.

Using my hip, I shoved it and nearly fell inside.

As I righted myself, I saw Ronald sitting behind a wooden desk.

It was obvious that his clients didn't often come here. This was definitely a workspace, one filled with overstuffed filing cabinets—I knew because all the drawers were open. An overflowing trashcan sat beside a desk without a visible inch of surface showing.

He stood, a stormy look on his face. "I'm not doing any interviews. How many times do I have to tell you people—" He paused and studied my face. "We've met before."

"I'm Holly. We met at the lunch for Travis put on by his parents."

"That's right." He pointed to a chair. "I'm sorry. I keep getting calls from reporters. Have a seat."

I did.

Ronald dropped his sausage biscuit back onto a greasy wrapper. "What can I do for you?"

I ignored what appeared to be a chunk of biscuit floating in the coffee cup in front of me. "I have some questions about Travis's death."

He raised his eyebrows. "PI?"

I shook my head. "Just stubborn and determined."

He chuckled, but the sound quickly faded. "I hope you're not coming here to question me. The police have already cleared me. I have an alibi for that night."

"I know. I'm not here to point a finger at you."

That seemed to help him relax. His shoulders slumped slightly. "So, how can I help?"

"You said you've worked with the Williams family for a long time. You sound like someone who knows the ins and outs of this business."

He nodded, looking more and more at ease. "I like to think I do."

"I'm just trying to understand how things operate.

Did Travis and Chuck ever work with anyone else while transporting bodies?" *Because if there was a third person, he could either be the next target or the killer.*

He reached for his coffee but his large hand knocked it over instead. Liquid spilled all over his papers and he muttered a few choice words. "No, those two were teammates to the end."

I watched as he grabbed some Kleenex to wipe up his mess. This man wasn't nearly organized enough to plan Travis's murder. This visit had already solidified that fact.

"What if it was a particularly large person?" I continued. "Might you need more people?"

"Everyone worked in twos to make it easier and for accountability. So, in a case like that, I would have sent another team there."

There went that lead. "How many teams do you have?"

"Three. And, before you ask, both of those teams were working on Saturday night. I went to help one of them. That was my alibi as well. My guys didn't do this."

"Good to know." I crossed and uncrossed my legs as I tried to gather my thoughts. "Why do you think someone would want to kill Travis?"

"I know that Travis liked to live beyond his means. He was in debt. And yet he still spent money. Who knows what kind of trouble that could lead to. Debt collectors? Loan sharks?"

He was the third person who'd mentioned Travis's potential debt. Interesting.

I needed to chew on that a little longer.

"Do you know why Chuck wasn't at the luncheon Travis's parents planned?"

"I heard he was already dead on Monday."

My stomach sank at the thought. I hadn't considered that the killer may have killed Travis and then immediately hunted down Chuck and killed him also. "You mentioned at the luncheon that Travis and Raul Williams had a fight last week. Do you know what it was about?"

"I have no idea."

"What do you know about Raul?"

"I know he's been bitter toward his brother for a long time."

His words sent surprise through me. "Toward Drew?"

He nodded. "Raul thought he should get the family business, but his grandfather didn't think he had a kind, compassionate enough spirit. It's caused some strife. Drew has always been the golden child while Raul had more of a wild streak."

"What's he been doing instead of working for the funeral home?"

"He started as a mortician. He even worked for another funeral home for a while. Then he tried to start a few of his own businesses, but I think they failed. Last I heard he was selling medical equipment. That's about all I can tell you."

Medical equipment. Could that somehow tie in with this? I didn't know.

Maybe he and Travis had some kind of side deal going on? Could they be writing fake invoices and pocketing the money?

I stood, knowing I'd gotten everything I could from this conversation. "Thank you. You've been very helpful."

I gripped my purse as I walked across the asphalt to my car.

As I did, I heard a car rev its engine behind me.

My shoulders tensed as I turned around to see what was happening.

That was when a sedan accelerated toward me.

CHAPTER 20

My gaze darted around me. All I saw were cement walls, orange doors, and asphalt. I had nowhere to run.

As the sedan sped toward me, instinct kicked in. I ran anyway. My heart pounded furiously in my ears with each footfall. What was going on?

Had the Texter followed me here? Was this how everything would end? Because I didn't see very many other alternatives.

My lungs squeezed as I pushed myself to go faster. It didn't matter.

My speed was no comparison to the oncoming vehicle.

I slowed for just long enough to grab one of the doors leading into a storage unit.

It was locked.

No! I'd known it was a long shot, but I didn't have a lot of options.

My hands trembled as I darted toward the next one.

It was also locked.

What was I going to do?

The car was going to ram into me at any minute.

I glanced down the street. One door in the distance was slightly cracked, like someone had forgotten to latch it. I had to make it there.

I lunged toward it and fell inside.

Just as I did, the car zoomed by outside, ripping the door off its hinges.

I tried to catch a glimpse of the vehicle. But the windows were tinted. I couldn't tell anything about the driver. I only knew it was a gray sedan—a Chevy—with Ohio plates.

Without getting up, I grabbed my phone and called Chase.

He showed up ten minutes later.

By then, I had pulled myself up from the dusty ground. My dress was now dirty, and my limbs were still shaking. Especially when I thought about how close I'd come to being hit. I'd only been seconds away.

"Are you okay?" He peered at me as we stood outside by the broken orange door. Crime-scene techs were gathering information on the tire tracks and taking flecks of some gray paint that had been scraped from the vehicle's door. I had little hope they'd come to any conclusions.

Was I okay? I got asked that question. A lot. "I suppose."

There was no way I could sell that sentiment trembling like I was.

"What were you even doing here?"

I swallowed hard, knowing how this would sound. "I stopped by to talk to Ronald Dillow."

He nodded slowly as realization spread over his

features. "I should have known."

I told him what I knew about the car, and he promised to check the security footage.

"There's one other thing you should know," Chase said. "We've been investigating that jewelry theft ring theory you told us about. You were right. Travis and Chuck were a part of it. We've gone to numerous pawnshops in the area and compared their inventory against those police reports."

"That's good news," I said. But why did I have a feeling there was more to this and that the "more" wasn't so good?

"As far as we can tell, Travis and Chuck were the only two involved," Chase continued.

"But if there was no one else involved, then who wanted them dead? A family member they stole from?" It just didn't make any sense. Then again, neither did all that money I'd found at Travis's place. We were missing something.

"We don't know yet. But we're still investigating."

"All the money at Travis's place doesn't make sense either. We're missing something."

"I agree." He paused. "By the way, I just wanted to say . . . good work."

I felt myself beaming a little. "Thanks."

***

I left work at 3:30 and decided to swing by the appliance store where I thought Jason Lewis worked. My elbow was still achy from my near run-in with death earlier. But I was happy to be alive.

I stepped inside the store and avoided the gazes of several salesmen who looked my way. I tried to find the man I'd seen in the fishing picture with Travis. Finally, I spotted someone who fit the bill. He just happened to be alone, not helping any customers. That was good news.

He smiled as I approached. "Welcome to Appliance Max, where you'll get the maximum value for a minimum price."

He was skinny—gawky almost—with dark hair and a goatee that needed to be trimmed. His dark hair only made his complexion look paler than it needed to be, and the ghastly lime-green polo shirt he wore didn't do anything to help.

"How can I help you?"

I offered my most winning grin. "I'm looking for a fridge—"

Before I could finish my sentence, recognition spread across his face—not good recognition, but angry, fearful recognition. "I've seen you before."

Well, that was a start.

"Have you?" I said, keeping my voice even.

He nodded and took a step back, his expression darkening and his gaze skittering. "What are you doing here?"

"Why do you look scared?" I asked.

He glanced around again, as if cops had surrounded the place. "Because I know who you are."

"Who am I?" I was confused now. He wasn't making any sense in word or deed.

His beady eyes met mine. "You're the girl Travis

picked."

Okay, this was getting stranger by the moment.

"I'm glad you brought that up. I need to know why he picked me as an online date. He obviously wasn't looking for his soulmate."

"He found himself in a pickle." He leaned against a stainless steel refrigerator and crossed his arms.

"Because he was stealing jewelry?"

His gaze clouded even more. "Well, it started as that."

I needed more information, and I needed it faster. "Jason, I really need to know what you know. Someone is trying to kill me. Please."

He glanced around before swallowing hard. "He started stealing jewelry to get some extra money around six months ago. I don't know what happened, but about three weeks ago, Travis changed. Something had gotten under his skin in a bad way, and he thought he might die."

Now we were getting somewhere. "He didn't say why or what happened?"

"No, he wouldn't tell me. But he read that article about you in the paper."

"The one about the crime ring I helped to bust a few months ago?"

He nodded. "That's the one. Anyway, Travis did a search for you online and found your profile on that winkable.com site. He decided to approach you there. It was like a God-given opportunity."

"Approach me about what?"

Jason shrugged. "Whatever was bothering him. He

said you could help."

So those texts he'd sent right before he died *weren't* intended for someone else. They were intended for me.

Interesting.

"Don't get me wrong—he thought you were gorgeous," Jason continued. "That's why he sent those photos to his parents. They'd been wanting him to settle down with a nice girl, and you fit the bill. Bing bang boom."

"Glad I could help with that," I said with an edge of sarcasm.

I'd never even met Travis, and he'd gotten me into a world of trouble. Thanks a lot.

"He was anxious to meet with you Saturday. He was hoping to have a chance to tell you something."

I was trying to follow this. I really was. But there was one thing that didn't make sense. "Why not tell the police?"

"Because they would have arrested him on the spot when they heard about the jewelry theft. You might have been able to actually help him without getting him into more trouble."

"Okay . . ." I wasn't sure if I was buying this or not. "You're certain you have no idea what else was going on?"

He glanced around again, that nervous look returning to his gaze. "He said he couldn't tell me. That it could get me killed. He told me I should go out of town also."

I shivered. "But now you're back?"

"I am. But I'm keeping my eyes wide open."

I let out a sigh and thought about what I should ask next. This was already a lot to comprehend. "Do you know anything about a key?"

"A key?" He looked clueless.

"Was there anywhere Travis liked to hang out where a mystery key might unlock something?"

"If Travis had a storage unit or cabin or anything else, he didn't tell me, if that's what you're asking."

That was exactly what I was asking.

"One more question and I'll go. Do you know anything about an argument Travis had with someone named Raul Williams?"

"The name sounds familiar, but, no, I can't say I do. I will tell you this: Travis was always getting caught in his lies. There's no telling what kind of trouble he got himself into. I'm kind of glad I don't know. And I plan on leaving town as soon as I can, just in case. Now, I need to get back to work. A possible commission just walked in."

He started toward a young couple that screamed newlyweds with their dreamy expressions and joined-at-the-hip demeanor.

I left a few minutes later. As soon as I stepped onto the sidewalk, someone grabbed my arm.

"We need to talk," he muttered.

I gasped when I recognized Raul Williams.

CHAPTER 21

Before I could react, Raul pulled me into the alcove of an old dress shop plastered with "For Lease" signs.

Panic raced through me. Everything happened at breakneck speed.

"What do you want with my brother?" he growled.

My eyes widened at his unexpected question. "What do you mean?"

His scowl deepened. "I went to Travis Hooker's memorial luncheon, and there were pictures of the two of you everywhere. Then my brother starts dating you a day later. What's going on?"

"It's a long story." I tried to take a step back, but I couldn't. The building was right behind me, and anyone walking past would probably think we were two lovers having a moment. Raul's broad shoulders blocked me from the crowd.

"I have time."

"Why don't you ask Drew?"

"I'm asking you." His teeth barely moved, only his lips. He was one scary guy.

"I never even met Travis," I blurted. "He made up the

story that we were dating. Okay? Are you happy now?"

He studied my face. "I don't trust you."

I stared back, a burst of courage coming to life inside me. "I don't trust you either. I know you were seen arguing with Travis last week. Maybe you're the one who should explain himself."

He narrowed his eyes. "I don't owe anyone an explanation."

"Nor do I, then. And I don't appreciate you tracking me down here and threatening me."

"I'm not threatening."

I raised my chin. "Then what are you doing?"

"I'm questioning."

"By cornering me? By trapping me?"

"You're free to go whenever you want." He scooted back, but only by a half a step.

So I stepped toward him half a step. "What are you hiding, Raul? Are you somehow trying to ruin your brother's business because you're bitter he took over instead of you?"

He sucked in a quick breath and released it just as quickly. "I would never do that."

"Well, you're obviously hiding something. In fact, maybe you're the one who's been following me. Who tried to run me down earlier. Who keeps sending me threatening texts, and who broke into my home."

He ran a hand over his face and his shoulders slumped. "Someone did that to you?"

"Yeah, someone did all that to me." I'd finally gotten through to him. Thank goodness.

"It wasn't me. And I didn't kill Travis. I discovered

what he was doing with the jewelry, and I told him he needed to come clean or I was going to take everything I knew to the police."

Maybe I was making some progress here. Finally. "How did he react to that?"

"Not well. He begged me to give him some time. He said he had some things he needed to clear up and then he'd fess up."

"And you agreed?"

Raul shrugged. "I gave him a week. He died five days later."

***

I climbed into my car to collect myself. Though the conversation with Raul had ended without drama, I was still reeling from his confrontation.

He'd claimed he'd come to see me at the office, but I'd left just as he was arriving. Instead, he'd followed me to Appliance Max and waited for me outside.

I still didn't have a good feel for the man. While I'd never felt my life had been directly in danger, his actions had been aggressive.

Was he somehow involved in this? Was he feeling me out to see what I knew?

I had no idea.

As Ella Fitzgerald crooned through my speakers, my phone rang. It was Ralph, and I assumed he was calling about work.

"I just ran into Chase," he said instead.

Something about the way he said the words made

tension stretch across my shoulders. If I wasn't careful, I was going to have permanently knotted muscles from all the stress I'd been under lately.

Ralph wasn't mentioning this casually. Not by a long shot.

"Did you? Where?"

"We both like the same bagel shop in Clifton," Ralph said. "But that's not why I'm calling. Chase mentioned something about a new roommate you had."

I closed my eyes and rubbed my neck. I knew where this conversation was going—a place I didn't wanted to venture into. Not right now. "Did he?"

"Stop responding with questions, Holly. He said she was your cousin. It took me a minute to realize what—or should I say who—he was talking about. You're letting Blake stay with you, aren't you?"

I didn't say anything, which was an answer within itself.

"Have you lost your mind?" His voice rose with exasperation.

Quite possibly. I didn't say that either. Instead, I said, "I was just trying to help her out."

"Letting a stranger stay with you isn't a good idea."

"It's no different than having a roommate. You and Alex already had all the background checks done on her, just like I would a roommate. It's all good."

He didn't say anything, but I knew he was fuming and trying to choose his words. "I don't like this, Holly. Having this woman stay with you is different. She's someone who's claiming to be related. If she's not telling the truth, then she's probably only come into our lives because she wants something, and who knows what that is."

Was my brother always so suspicious? I didn't think so. But he sounded awfully paranoid now. "I appreciate your concern, but I can assure you I'm being cautious."

Another moment of silence stretched as Ralph unleashed his big brother protectiveness. "Chase also said someone broke into your house the other night."

I leaned my head back against the seat. "Well, isn't he just a little tattletale."

My words were supposed to be humorous, but Ralph obviously didn't take them that way.

"He assumed I knew." It sounded like Ralph had said the words through gritted teeth.

It took a lot to get my diplomatic, even-keeled brother this fired up. I'd somehow achieved that. As a little sister, I had a knack for doing that.

"He assumed wrong," I said.

"Why didn't you tell me?"

"Because I've got the situation under control." Even as I said the words, I realized the fallacy of them. Did I ever have things totally under control? No.

"You obviously don't," Ralph pointed out.

Okay, so even though I knew that, he didn't have to remind me. I was quickly growing weary of this conversation. "Ralph, what's your point? Why are you calling?"

"You need to get this woman to move out before it turns ugly. There have been some weird legal cases where tenants claim ownership of property, and the court has ruled in their favor. They're nearly impossible to evict and can make the owners' lives miserable."

"I think you're overreacting." Which was so unlike him. Which made me think that I should possibly consider his words.

"Holly . . . please. For once in your life, listen to your older brother."

A new heaviness settled on my chest. "I'm not making any promises. But I'll think about it."

"Please do that. And quickly."

***

I got back to work and, out of curiosity, hopped on my computer. I searched for any news articles concerning Travis's death. There were several, but none shed any light on the investigation.

Finally, I found some photos that had been posted by bystanders who were there that evening. I began scrolling through them, examining the people there.

I stopped at one and squinted.

That couldn't be right . . . could it?

I enlarged the photo so I could see it better.

Sure enough, there was Jason Lewis in the crowd.

He hadn't been in Wisconsin after all.

I bit down, chewing on that thought. The only reason he'd lie would be if he was hiding something.

Before I could call Chase about it, my phone rang.

It was my mom. She must be back from Florida finally. I knew I had to take the call because we had a lot to talk about.

I pushed the thoughts of Jason aside as I answered,

"Hey, Mom. Welcome home."

We chitchatted a few minutes. Inevitably, the subject of Blake came up.

"What do you think of this young lady?" Mom asked. "Did you like her? What sense about her did you get?"

I chose my words wisely. I tried to, at least. "She seems to be a bit of a partier. She said she has a good family life. Her dad's a farmer."

"That's good to know."

"But, Mom, I'm still trying to figure out how she found us. Did you post an ad on an online forum on adoption?"

Silence stretched for a minute. "I did. I posted a message on this online group with details of your father's birth. I was hoping to connect with his birth family."

"I'm not going to lie—I'm surprised. Why would you do that? It seems unlike you."

"I don't know." Her voice cracked. "I just thought it could be one last gift to give your father."

I wasn't sure, but it almost sounded like she was crying.

I knew she was trying to move on. She'd even started dating someone. But maybe she missed Dad more than she'd let on.

Wasn't that what we were all doing? Trying to move on while still honoring the memories of those who'd passed away? The balancing act could be difficult.

"Did you get any responses?" I asked.

"No, I didn't. I was just going to let it go." She paused. "I would like to meet her."

"I'll see what I can arrange," I said.

As I hung up, my thoughts continued to churn. I couldn't just sit here, not when the answers were out there.

I wanted to go back to that pawnshop again. The man behind the counter had seen the people selling this jewelry. I felt certain he had more information than he'd let on.

CHAPTER 22

Jamie and I headed back to the pawnshop. The same man was working behind the counter. I could only assume he owned the place.

He sneered when he saw us. "You two again?"

"We really need information," I started. "I need to know whom you bought that jewelry from. It's important. My life is in danger," I said, trying to appeal to the masculine, protective side that every man had buried deep down inside . . . right?

"Don't know. Gave me a fake driver's license."

I flinched. "Really?"

"That's what I hear." He scowled. "You happy now? One got by me. You know I lose money for stuff like this. The police come and confiscate it, and I'm the one who loses out."

"Can I see that driver's license?" I asked.

"The police took the copy of it," he said.

"Can you describe this person then?" Jamie said.

"Not really."

"Do you have security cameras?" I nodded toward the ones above me.

"They're just there for show. They don't work."

Someone bustled from the office. My eyes widened when I recognized the woman with the beehive hairdo.

Gladys from the choir at Community Church.

"Holly?" Her mouth formed an O. "I never expected to see you here. You don't strike me as the pawnshop type."

"Nor do you," I said.

She placed her hand on the man's arm. "This is Frankie. He's my son."

She beamed up at her offspring, like he was her proudest accomplishment, even with his stained T-shirt and dirty teeth. A mother's love knew no bounds.

"Frankie, are you giving these ladies a hard time?"

His shoulders sank, like that which could only happen under a mother's scrutiny. "Of course not, Mom."

"What brings the two of you in here?" she asked.

"We're trying to figure out who brought some stolen jewelry here."

"I hate to say it, but that happens all the time. We try to go through everything first and make sure things are on the up and up. But it's easy for things to slip past."

"This is really important, though," I said. "You see, someone is trying to kill me, and I need to identify who it is before this person succeeds."

She gasped and took a step back. "Oh, you poor dear. Why would anyone want to kill someone with a voice as angelic as yours?"

"That's a great question. Apparently, I've made them mad."

"Frankie, you can't let someone try to kill her. Go get that video footage."

His shoulders sank even further, as if he knew he was buried.

"I thought the cameras didn't work?" I looked at Frankie point-blank.

His eyes narrowed and his jaw set. "I only use that for my own purposes. Not for the police."

"I'm not the police."

"No one's going to want to do business with me if I'm a nark."

His mom swatted him on the arm. "You don't do business with people like that, Frankie. Didn't I teach you better? Now go get that footage."

"Yes, Mother."

He disappeared into the back, walking like a dog that had just been beaten. I couldn't even feel sorry for him, though.

"He's a nice boy. He really is." Her eyes lit. "And he's single . . ."

I realized her implications and took a step back. "I'm seeing someone."

I'd been on the fence about Drew, but this decided it. We were seeing each other, even if it was just temporarily.

"That's too bad, but I should have figured." Her gaze went to Jamie.

My friend shook her head and took a step back. "Oh, no. My family . . . they don't believe in pawnshops. They'd disown me."

Ms. Gladys squinted but seemed to accept Jamie's

answer.

Just then, Frankie came back in, carrying a small laptop computer. He placed it on the counter, his lips still snarled in a scowl.

"Here's the person who sold this," he said, turning the screen toward us.

I held my breath, waiting to see if this was the clue I needed to push this case over the edge.

I watched the footage. It was grainy, but I hoped I'd be able to make out enough of what I saw.

A moment later, a figure came onto the screen.

I sucked in a deep breath.

It was a woman, and she had auburn hair that was long with a gentle curl.

She looked like me.

Or should I say, she looked like Blake.

***

I dreaded going back to my place. Mostly because I knew I'd run into Blake and, when I ran into her, that we needed to have an uncomfortable conversation. I hated uncomfortable conversations like some people hated eating brussels sprouts.

But I did have some questions for Blake that had to be addressed. First of all, I wanted to know about her timing. Was it a coincidence that she showed up here right as all of this was happening? I also wanted to know about her hair. Had she purposefully changed it to look like mine?

I asked Frankie about the driver's license the

woman had given him when dropping off the jewelry. Though he no longer had a copy of it, he said that the woman's hair was different in that photo. She'd told him she decided to try a new hair style recently.

When I pulled into my driveway, I saw Blake's car parked on the street and two lights on in the windows of the house. She was here. There was no turning back now.

Before I could slip out of the car and begin the dreaded trek toward the House of Confrontation, my phone rang. It was Drew. I welcomed the chance to procrastinate, so I answered. But Raul jumped to the forefront of my thoughts. Did Drew know his brother had talked to me? If not, should I mention it?

"Hey," I said.

"Hey, Holly. How's it going?"

My knotted stomach loosened a bit when I heard his voice.

We shared a few minutes of chitchat.

I didn't share much about Travis. I wasn't ready to.

"Listen, can I tempt you into going to dinner again tomorrow night?" Drew asked. "I mean, you've got to eat, right? Why not eat with me?"

I leaned back and smiled again. He was persistent, which wasn't necessarily a bad thing. I wanted a guy in my life who would fight to be with me, who wasn't afraid to go after what he wanted.

After all, Chase had walked away.

That realization caused my gut to twist again.

"Dinner? Really?" It wasn't the most intelligent thing I could have said.

"I think modern dating etiquette would tell me I should wait a few more days before I called and asked you, but I decided I didn't care."

A man who knew the rules of etiquette? That was amazing.

I could see where it would be very easy for Drew to edge his way into my life . . . and into my heart. That was a fact I needed to be very mindful of. "Let's do dinner then. It would be nice."

"Excellent. There's this little hole-in-the-wall—"

"I love hole-in-the-wall places."

"I was hoping you might." He rattled off the address, and we said goodbye with a promise to see each other the next day.

Twice in one week? I was surprising even myself. But I offered myself another stark reminder to be careful. Sometimes when people seemed too good to be true, it was because they were.

I had to carefully consider whether or not Drew could be a part of this. I didn't want to believe it, but I didn't want to be stupid, either.

With that conversation done, I had no excuse to stay in the car. I had to go inside and have an honest conversation with Blake. I couldn't put it off any longer.

I clutched my keys in my hands as I walked across the cracked sidewalk leading to my front door. *Dear Lord, please help me to find the right words to say. If Blake is the real deal, I don't want to scare her off or offend her.*

When I climbed the three steps leading to my stoop, I was surprised to find the door unlocked.

I needed to have a conversation with Blake about the crime rate in this area. Certainly she should have realized that it wasn't very safe. Though I believed in living by faith not fear, unlocked doors were just asking for trouble.

I stepped inside, locked the door, and glanced around. Blake wasn't at her normal place on the couch, although her laptop and textbooks were sprawled there, almost as if she'd just left. Maybe she'd run to the bathroom.

"Hello?" I called, placing my purse and keys on the table by the entryway. "Blake, I'm home."

I still didn't hear anything. I walked deeper into the house, expecting to hear a hairdryer or flushing toilet.

I heard nothing.

I paced down the hallway. I checked each room. I didn't see her anywhere.

Maybe she was in the backyard. The evening was nice and temperate, so maybe she'd stepped outside for a breather during a study break.

I pushed open the old metal screen door, one that I wanted to replace sometime soon. I stepped onto the deck. "Blake?"

Silence.

I scanned my surroundings. Everything was in place. The little table in the corner with two wicker chairs. A small grill with a tight-fitting cover. A small expanse of grass with a pink dogwood tree in the corner, one that just happened to be flowering right now.

Where had she gone?

As I considered the possibilities, an ice-cold feeling

settled in my gut.

CHAPTER 23

I paced my house, giving Blake the chance to magically reappear. All the possible excuses as to where she might be raced through my mind.

Maybe she'd stepped outside for a walk. Maybe a friend had come by and picked her up. Maybe . . . I had a million other reasons why she could be gone right now.

But none of them quite rang true, not when I added all the facts together.

What if she'd figured out I was onto her, and she'd left before I could ask more questions? But, if that was the case, she would have taken her purse. Her phone. Her car.

All those things were still here.

And that fact disturbed me.

On the other hand, there was no sign of forced entry. There was nothing to indicate a struggle had taken place here. It almost looked like she'd just upped and left.

Finally, I grabbed my phone from my purse and stopped my insane stepping. Enough was enough. I needed to call Chase.

He showed up ten minutes later, and my heart did that familiar tugging and tingling dance that always threw me off-balance. And when I saw that familiar worry in his eyes, the dance happened again.

Chase just had that effect on me. But that didn't mean we were meant to be. Slowly, that was starting to sink in.

"What's going on?" he asked.

I opened my mouth to respond. I tried to answer him. I wanted to. I really did.

But he was wearing a white button-up shirt, and he looked like he'd just come from a nice dinner. And there was lipstick on his collar.

My eyes wouldn't leave it. Had I interrupted him from a date?

"Everything okay, Holly?" he asked.

I wanted to ask questions. To demand answers. But that wasn't my right. And I had no room to talk or complain. I'd gone out with Drew.

Despite my logic, a small part of my heart felt battered.

I cleared my throat, pulled my gaze away from that lipstick stain, and pushed those thoughts aside. Tried to at least. And then I told Chase what I knew.

"Have you tried to call Blake?" Chase asked.

"Yes, but her phone is here."

He grunted in thought. A hand went to his hip, and he glanced around. "You said the front door was unlocked?"

I nodded. "But nothing seems disturbed. I just don't understand."

"Okay, let's sit down and talk this through."

A few minutes later, I'd made coffee, and Chase and I sat at the kitchen table. He had his pad and paper out to take notes.

He asked me tons of questions about Blake, and I felt as if I'd repeated the information over and over without sharing anything new. I knew he had to go through this process in order to find her, but it didn't make it any less frustrating.

With every passing minute, I was more and more convinced that something had happened to her. Something bad.

Was Blake somehow connected with this whole ordeal? What about the pawnshop? Why had she been there?

"Holly, you look like you're beside yourself," Chase said.

I shook my head and realized I'd stood and begun pacing. "I just keep thinking that I've got my act together, and then everything falls apart."

"You're the most together person I know."

"I don't feel together." I especially didn't feel that way lately. "I feel like trouble is following me everywhere I go. I have no idea what to do about it. Not to even mention the fact that I have no clue as to why Blake would be snatched. I mean, she checks out. She is who she said she was. My brother and sister looked into it."

"But that doesn't mean she's related. You won't know that until you do a DNA test."

"But why would she lie?" Chase started to answer

when I shook my head. "Never mind. I already know. Alex and Ralph also went over that with me. There are numerous reasons."

"One of the things I've always loved about you is that you think the best of people, Holly."

"Thinking the best of people is going to get me killed, isn't it?"

"Not if I have anything to do with it."

"But, Chase, you can't always be around me." My eyes went to that lipstick stain again.

I didn't care. That's what I tried to tell myself. It was no big deal, and it was none of my business.

But deep inside, I cared. I really cared.

Oh, Holly, get a grip.

Finally, Chase stood. "I've got the information I need, and I'll see what I can do. With no evidence of foul play, it's going to be a little harder to get things moving in a timely manner."

I followed him to the door, where he paused.

Great. Another awkward goodbye.

"Holly, there's one other thing that I think is worth mentioning," Chase started.

I nodded and waited for him to continue. I didn't like the tone of his words. Something about the way he said them made my spine tighten and squeeze.

"We need to consider the idea that someone snatched Blake, thinking she was you."

The blood drained from my face. "What? No, that's ridiculous."

Chase shook his head, his eyes narrowing with a mix of compassion and austerity. "Holly, from behind, the two of you look alike. She's staying in your house. There's a good chance you were the target tonight."

***

"Oh, girlfriend. It's been a long time since we've done a road trip together," Jamie said.

I'd taken off work, and Jamie and I were visiting Hillsboro.

I needed to learn more about Blake. If she was my cousin, I wanted to meet her family. If she wasn't my cousin, I wanted to talk to her family about her disappearance and find out why she might have made this up.

Doing this was the next logical step in finding answers.

I gripped my steering wheel. It may be cliché, but I'd tied a pretty pink scarf around my hair. We were driving with the windows open, and my hair was flying like crazy. I'd also slipped on some oversized sunglasses.

Along the country road, spring bloomed and green surrounded us. Rolling hills beckoned exploration or pictures. Maybe even some stargazing at night.

We were in my Mustang, and, for Jamie's sake, I'd switched from Bing Crosby to Harry Connick Jr. He worked in a pinch. I needed a day off and I needed some answers. Time was of the essence.

We were almost to Hillsboro, which was a little more than an hour away from home, and my nerves wanted to get the best of me. It was a small town. Jamie and I, most likely, would stand out. If we asked too many questions, people would get suspicious. But I desperately wanted some answers, and I had no idea where to start in my quest for finding Blake back in Cincinnati.

Part of me didn't want to meet Blake's family. I wanted to pretend they didn't exist. I didn't want to see the heartbreak in their eyes. See the possible suspicion when I told them about everything that had transpired.

But I was here. And I needed to do this.

We pulled up to a farm thirty minutes later. It really was beautiful. There were more rolling hills. A lovely white farmhouse. Two big barns and several long white buildings—chicken houses, maybe?—in the background. Fields of some sort that were just beginning to sprout.

A dog ran up the lane to greet us, barking merrily, and, before I'd even cut the engine, a man and woman were standing on the porch, watching us. I wasn't sure if they were the welcoming committee or the firing squad. I guessed I'd figure it out in a minute.

I waved as I stepped from my car and gently shut the door. I smoothed my dress and stole a glance at Jamie. She nodded toward them, indicating she'd follow my lead.

"Hello," I called as I came up the walk. "I'm sorry to stop by so unexpectedly. I'm Holly Paladin."

They didn't show any recognition of my name, so either they hadn't heard it from Blake or they were great actors.

"How can we help you?" the woman asked.

"I'm here from Cincinnati, and I have a couple of questions."

"You're here about Blake?" Mr. Hallowell stared at me, waiting for a response.

I had to admit that I was surprised he didn't have a more emotional response. Most people in a situation like this would be nearly devastated or at least beside themselves with worry.

I nodded. "That's right."

"The sheriff just came by and told us," Mrs. Hallowell said.

"I'm so sorry," I said. "I can't imagine what you're going through."

They didn't say anything.

Could these people actually be my relatives? It was a strange thought.

"Why don't you have a seat?" the woman said. "Can I get you some lemonade?"

"I'd actually love some." I paused at the base of the wooden steps leading to the gorgeous wraparound porch.

A moment later, Jamie and I were situated on the peeling metal chairs and the Hallowells sat on a cheerful yellow swing. Introductions went around. The woman was Regina and her husband was Lloyd. Regina had a pleasant but plain face with salt-and-pepper hair that had been pulled back in a harsh pony tail. Lloyd had white hair that was slightly frizzy on the edges around his neck. He had a middle-aged pouch and watchful eyes.

"Blake talked about how much she loved it here," I

started, gripping my sweaty glass and praying I could find the right words. I didn't know what was going on with Blake, but I feared she might be in trouble right now. Because of me.

"Did she?" Mr. Hallowell rocked back and forth on a squeaky-chained swing.

"And about all the different egg dishes you would make," I continued.

"Farm living." Regina smiled sadly.

Something about their reactions weren't jiving with me, but I reminded myself that everyone handled trauma differently. Just because I couldn't relate to their actions didn't mean they were wrong.

I licked my lips. "I'm so sorry about everything that's happened."

"How did you say you knew Blake?" Lloyd shifted, his drink still untouched.

"She came to find me," I said. "She told me that we could be related. That her grandmother had given a baby up for adoption nearly sixty years ago."

Regina stared at me, her expression unreadable. "Is that right?"

"I hope I'm not springing this on you. You did already know, didn't you?"

They exchanged a glance.

"It's a long story," Regina said.

Something was wrong here. They weren't reacting like a normal person might. These were big revelations to be sharing, and they seemed unaffected beyond reason.

I was suddenly more than a little uncomfortable.

"We should go." I stood, unable to ignore my unease any longer. "Thanks for the lemonade."

"Wait!" Lloyd said. "Please."

I paused halfway down the steps.

"Please forgive us for letting you go through all these questions," Regina said. "I wanted to know more, however."

"More about Blake's disappearance?" She wasn't making sense to me.

"You could say that." Regina exchanged a glance with her husband. "There's something you should know."

"What's that?" I braced myself, sensing the revelation would be big.

"Blake, come out here," she called.

I held my breath. Had Blake been here the whole time? I didn't know whether to be relieved or angry.

But the woman who stepped out onto the porch wasn't the Blake I'd met before.

It looked like I'd been scammed . . . again.

CHAPTER 24

"That was rough," Jamie said, a dazed expression on her face.

"More than rough," I muttered, knowing my expression reflected hers.

I was letting Jamie drive my Mustang back to Cincinnati from Hillsboro, something that I never did. I was pretty protective of my car. Sadly so, at times. But I was flustered right now, and I knew my focus was gone.

"Blake Hallowell wasn't really Blake Hallowell," I said, playing with the end of a curly strand of hair. "What in the world is going on?"

"I have no idea. It's all getting too weird for me."

I chewed on my thoughts still, rubbing the ends of my hair against my jaw. Not even Harry Connick Jr. was cheering me up right now. "Was she working with Travis and Chuck? Is she the ringleader?"

"Maybe. But why? What's her connection?"

"I have no idea. There's something we're missing, Jamie."

"I agree. I just don't know what."

When I laid out the facts and stripped everything else away, the answer suddenly seemed obvious. My

Blake was using an assumed identity. Travis and Chuck were stealing something from dead people. Put that together and you had . . .

"ID theft," I muttered.

"What?"

A surge of excitement rushed through me. "What if the three of them—Blake, Travis, and Chuck—were stealing the IDs of the people who died? Maybe sneaking their Social Security cards—or asking for their numbers as verification when they signed the bodies out? That would put them in the perfect position to steal someone's identity."

Jamie wagged her head thoughtfully. "Maybe."

"We know it's something bigger than jewelry. This could be the answer we've been looking for."

"I'm not denying it. But wouldn't there be easier ways to do that? Like on a computer?"

"I have no idea." My hands flew in the air. "But I feel like we're onto something, Jamie. Like we're really onto something."

As I said the words, my hand hit one of my earrings, and it flew off. I groaned. Go figure. The one time I act with histrionics, I lose one of my favorite pieces of jewelry.

I reached between my seats to try and retrieve it. I felt around on the carpet, trying to find it through touch since I couldn't see anything.

My fingers felt something smooth with hard edges wedged beneath the driver's seat.

That wasn't my earring. But what was it?

I finally got a good grip on it and jerked my hand

out.

I stared at the object I held.

It appeared to be a jump drive, one I'd never seen before.

"Where did that come from?" Jamie glanced away from the road for a second.

I slowly let the air out of my lungs, a touch of satisfaction washing over me. I studied it one more minute to confirm my initial thoughts. "I think this used to be attached to that keychain that someone stuck in my pocket. The metal end fit right here. It must have fallen out somehow. The key was never significant. This was."

Jamie and I exchanged a glance.

"We've got to get this to Chase." I pulled out my phone and wasted no time.

If Blake was involved, this didn't matter. But if she was an innocent bystander, this discovery could mean the difference between life and death.

***

I dropped Jamie off at home—her mom had a babysitting situation and needed Jamie there ASAP—and then I hurried to the police station.

Chase escorted me to his office and shut the door behind us. I handed him the jump drive, feeling giddier than a bride about to walk down the aisle.

I couldn't wait to find out what was on this device

"I can't believe this was in your car," he muttered, sitting at his desk.

"I know. Me neither."

Chase studied it as he walked toward his desk. He sat and inserted the device into his computer. Whatever was on this jump drive had made my life precariously miserable. Maybe all of this would finally end. A girl could hope.

The computer slowly loaded. I stood behind him, not wanting to miss a thing.

I held my breath as I waited to see what would pop up on the screen. Finally, a list of numbers appeared. They were listed in three columns with no text.

Chase and I both stared at the screen.

Some of my excitement evaporated as more questions stared me in the face. Nothing was ever easy, was it?

"Any idea what this means?" I leaned closer for a better look.

"I have no idea." He pointed to the first column. "Maybe this is an invoice number?"

"The second column could be Social Security numbers."

"It's the correct amount of digits. And what if that third column is a payment amount?"

"Okay, maybe we're getting somewhere with this."

"Could this be money people have made through selling other people's identities?" I asked.

I explained to him what I'd learned about Blake.

Chase leaned back with a sigh. "It's within the realm of possibility. And if that last column is the amount people are making on this, it would be reason enough for someone to kill. If we're right, someone is raking in thousands of dollars."

I walked around his desk and sat down in the chair on the other side. "So, whoever is behind this should have money. Should have access to people who've recently died. Should be smart. Have connections."

Raul? He was the first person who came to mind. Because even if Blake was involved, she had to be working with someone. After all, it was a man who'd broken into my house. A man who'd tried to steal my purse.

But I couldn't deny that Drew fit that description also. I didn't want to believe it, but it was true.

"Travis and Chuck must have collected this information," Chase said. "Maybe they were going to go to the police with it, and the ringleader found out about their plan. Whoever is behind this must know that this information can bring him down. He'd not only lose money but he'd face jail time."

I rubbed my temples, feeling a headache coming on. "What do we do now?"

"I'm going to let my tech guys look at this. We'll run some of these numbers to confirm our theory. Until then, you should play it safe."

Should I tell him that I had a date with Drew this evening?

No, maybe I shouldn't.

Maybe I should cancel, for that matter.

I didn't know.

But Drew couldn't be behind this. He'd been with me when I'd gotten a couple of those texts.

I replayed the scene at the Mediterranean restaurant

when I'd gotten the message that made it clear the bad guy knew I was eating hummus. Drew's hands had been concealed behind the menu at some point. Had he been able to compose that text and then send it while he spoke with me?

But then that man had tried to snatch my purse while Drew was there. Drew hadn't been able to catch him. But what if that had been on purpose? What if Drew had hired someone to take my purse?

I didn't want to believe any of this. But I didn't want to be stupid either.

Chase's gaze caught mine. As if he could read my mind, he said, "You know Drew could be involved."

I nodded, wishing my head would stop spinning.

"What are you going to do about it?"

Was he asking me if I was going to continue to date Drew?

I squirmed. "I don't know, Chase."

"I don't want to see you get hurt." His voice sounded grim and serious, perfectly matching his gaze.

Was he talking about getting killed or Drew breaking my heart? I had no idea.

"Just tread with caution, okay?" Chase said.

"I will." Melancholy laced my words. "And Chase? What does all this mean for Blake? Will you continue to look for her?"

"Absolutely. It's just that right now, we don't know what side of the law she's on concerning this."

"I understand."

When I left ten minutes later, I knew exactly what I needed to do. I needed to keep my date with Drew. And

I needed to find out all the information I could.

***

When Chase had looked away from the computer earlier, I'd taken a photo of the screen using my phone. I wanted a copy of information that was important enough that two people had died. Yet I felt guilty again obtaining it this way. I shouldn't have done it, yet I needed that information if I was going to figure this out. My life was on the line here as well. I had a stake in this.

I wondered if Drew knew what these numbers might mean. I had to be wise with my next moves so I wouldn't get myself killed.

But I really wanted to ask him. I was going to have to trust my gut and play this by ear.

And why hadn't the Texter texted me lately? Had he given up? Had he moved on?

Would I be that lucky?

Drew called me as I drove home, told me he was running late, and asked if I could meet him at the funeral home instead of Bertie's.

Alicia met me at the door. "Mr. Williams is waiting for you in the back. I was just getting ready to leave, but he asked me to let you in."

"Sorry to keep you here late on a Friday night."

She shrugged. "It's no problem. I don't have any big plans anyway."

I stepped out of the brisk weather. A thunderstorm was blowing in, and it felt like it would be a doozy.

"This way," Alicia said, indicating with her hand that

244

I should follow.

"So, how'd you stumble into this business?" I asked as we strolled beside each other.

"I used to date Drew's brother, believe it or not."

Raul? I couldn't see him being warm and caring enough to date anyone. "And it's not awkward to work here?"

"His family is pretty great. They still accept me, even if I'm not directly connected."

"I see."

"And my father used to be a mortician, so I kind of know the ins and the outs of this business."

Alicia didn't seem as perky right now—her steps were slow, her words sounded dull.

As we stepped into the hallway, I paused. "Is everything okay?"

She offered a smile, but it looked forced. "It's just been one of those days."

"I'd guess that this job can wear on you."

She nodded but looked unconvinced still.

"And then with everything that's happened lately . . . with Travis and Chuck. That only adds to your stress," I prodded.

"Absolutely." She released a quick breath. "Holly, can I tell you something?"

"Of course."

"I shouldn't dump this on you. But you seem so nice. And I can't tell anyone here. I don't know whom to talk to."

"What's going on, Alicia?"

She glanced around, as if to make sure no one was

listening, before whispering, "Someone at Wilford has a PO box."

I wasn't quite understanding where she was going with this. "Okay . . ."

"I wasn't supposed to know," she continued. "But when I was coming to unlock the door for you, I found this envelope on the floor with the PO box address on it. I have no idea who dropped it."

"Did you open it?"

She bit down before shaking her head. "It was just the envelope. Nothing was inside."

"You have no idea who it came from?"

She shook her head. "No idea. But there's no reason for someone here to have a PO box, Holly. Unless they're hiding something. Maybe something . . . illegal."

My back muscles pinched with tension at her implications. "Who would do that? Why?"

"I have no idea. It makes me wonder if someone is profiting off the operations at the home."

Her words caused my breath to catch. Could this be another clue? Were these crimes based around the funeral home? "Do you have any idea what kind of operations that might be?"

She shrugged and stepped closer. "I'm not sure what's going on, Holly. But I'm scared."

"You think your life is in danger?"

"I wasn't supposed to know about the PO box. I handle a lot of the bookkeeping around here. I'm the one person who has the knowledge of day-to-day operations here. I'm the person who could easily bring all of this crashing down."

"That makes sense."

"There have been a lot of whispered conversations around here lately. I guess they're what put the idea in my head that something isn't right."

"Whispered conversations between whom?" I asked.

"Raul and Drew."

***

To say I had reservations about being here would be an understatement. Alicia led me toward the back, to an area of the funeral home that I'd never seen. I tried to make small talk, even though my mind was racing.

Alicia paused outside a room in the back. "It can be a little jarring the first time," she warned.

I could only imagine. "Thanks for the heads up."

"Good luck." She pushed the door open and announced my arrival. "And please don't tell anyone what I told you."

I sucked in a deep breath—totally second-guessing myself—but then stepped inside the sterile room anyway. I blanched when I saw the dead body, partially covered with a sheet. I had a feeling that sheet had been put there for me and no other reason.

"Holly," Drew said.

He wore something that reminded me of doctor's scrubs. It was a very different look than what I was used to, and it temporarily threw me off-balance.

"Thanks for letting Holly in, Alicia," he called over his shoulder.

"No problem." Alicia threw me a sympathetic smile

before she stepped out.

I glanced around at the cement walls. A huge metallic box was center right in the room. Everything appeared so sterile and almost like a hospital room. It kind of gave me the creeps.

"This is too much for you, isn't it?" Drew asked, looking away from the paper in his hands.

It was, but I didn't tell him that. "No, I'm . . . good."

He grinned. "You can tell the truth."

"This is kind of creepy." Right on cue, thunder rumbled overhead.

"That's a normal reaction, I assure you." He raised his paper. "I'm just finishing up. I'm sorry that you had to meet me here. Maybe I should have canceled, but I was really looking forward to seeing you."

"It's good to see you also." *Unless you're a killer.*

I shivered at the thought. I didn't want to believe it.

"So, you have to prep a body before a cremation?" I started, trying to turn my thoughts away from the morbidness of murder. Talking about death wasn't much better. But maybe I would get some insight into Travis or Chuck.

"That's right. I have to make sure there are no pacemakers or anything that could pop in the crematory and create dangerous conditions."

"How long does that process take?" I asked, unsure if I really wanted to know.

"Usually about three hours. Then you have to let the remains cool. After a magnet is used to take away any metal screws from the coffin. The remains also have to be put through a cremator."

"What's that?"

"It's a processor that will grind the bones up into an even finer consistency so we can give the ashes to loved ones."

"I see." I swallowed hard.

"This man, once 230 pounds, will be reduced to about five pounds." He paused. "Is this too much for you?"

"No . . . well, maybe. I'm still not sure."

He offered a lopsided grin. "You've made it further than most people."

"I'll be sure to bring that up next time I run out of things to talk about with my family."

He chuckled. "You're funny."

I drew in a deep breath, hoping we could get out of here soon.

"Any updates on the investigation?" Drew asked, sliding the body back into a refrigerated holding area.

I told him a little bit about Blake and what I'd discovered today. I wasn't sure if I'd tell him about the jump drive. Probably not. But maybe.

I wanted to trust him. I really did.

"How about you?" I asked. "Did you hear anything more about Travis or Chuck?"

"No, I haven't. But I've had reporters calling. This isn't what we need here."

Because reputation was important to him. Important enough that he would try to silence anyone who tarnished his shine? I didn't know.

"I still can't believe the lengths Travis was going through, though," Drew said. "Stealing jewelry from dead people? I'm ashamed for him, and I'm grieving for the families who've had only more heartache during such difficult times."

"Are you still using the same company? Dillow's?"

His cheek twitched. The action was so small that I almost missed it. "I am."

"But . . ." I started, wondering what he was thinking.

He looked up at me, surprise in his eyes. "But what?"

"You look unconvinced that you made a good choice."

He crossed his arms. "You read that on me?"

"I did. Am I right?"

"I suppose I'm a bit gun-shy. Too many screw-ups like this could greatly damage the reputation of my family's business. My grandfather worked so hard for this. I don't want to be the one who ruins it."

That seemed like an honorable reason. But all my doubts tried to crowd my logic.

Drew stepped closer. "You're a good listener, Holly."

"I try." The look in his eyes showed admiration and attraction. That was when a terrible thought hit me. *Please don't try to kiss me in a crematory. I'll never get over it. I won't.*

"It's late, isn't it?" He looked away as if he could read my thoughts.

I nodded. "I suppose it is."

"Let me get cleaned up, and then we can grab a bite to eat. Okay?"

The sooner I was out of here, the better. "Sounds great."

"Oh, and the bathroom door is broken. Just in case

you suddenly have the urge to go, don't."

"I'll keep that in mind."

***

As Drew got changed, I wandered around the funeral home. I couldn't help but feel like all the ghosts of funerals past were lurking around me, haunting me with just as much fervor as my uncertainties about this case. On a rational level, I knew this was irrational. But on an emotional level, I was spooked. I didn't ever want to become comfortable here.

I supposed it could have been the events of the past year that had me feeling this way. It could be the fact that it was night time. Maybe it was even because of the thunderstorm rumbling outside. All those things majorly played on my emotions right now.

I finally gave up on my pacing. I sat in a padded chair against the wall, no doubt where many mourners had sat before. The storm continued to rage outside and thunder rumbled, shaking the building.

There was really nothing good about being in a funeral home in the evening during a storm.

I shivered.

Maybe I shouldn't have come here tonight. Maybe all of this was a bad idea.

I should have canceled. Run for my life.

I just didn't know whom I could trust anymore.

Lightning flashed outside, deepening my chill.

My throat felt tight as I stood and walked toward the door, checking to see if the streets were starting to flood.

I'd only taken a few steps when lightning lit the sky again.

A figure stood at the front door.

I gasped and froze.

This person simply stood. Lurked. Watched.

Fear instantly crippled me.

CHAPTER 25

I backed away from the door, nearly stumbling on nothing but fear itself.

I had to do something before that man got inside.

But my mind froze.

My eyes wouldn't leave the silhouette.

Who was it? The killer? Had he come to finish what he'd started? To live out his threats?

It was my best guess. I couldn't bear to think about it.

Do something, Holly!

My mind raced. I should call for Drew.

I opened my mouth, but my voice had disappeared—gone right along with my logic.

Just then, my phone buzzed. I grabbed it and glanced at the screen. My hands trembled so badly that I could hardly read the words there.

It was Chase.

I answered. But before I could tell him about the man at the door, he rushed ahead of me.

"Holly, we just got the tox results back," he said. "I knew it was urgent that I tell you this."

"Tell me what?" I stared at the door, waiting for more lightning so I could see if the man was still there or not.

But it remained dark outside.

I needed to move, I realized. If he had a gun, I was setting myself up as a target.

I ducked closer to the wall and out of sight.

"Both Travis and Chuck were injected with a mix of chemicals," Chase said. "The majority was arsenic. That's what ultimately killed them. But there were also traces of something else."

"What?"

"Formaldehyde."

My throat went dry. "Formaldehyde?"

"That's right. It's used in embalming fluid."

"So, you think . . .?" The words lodged in my throat as facts stormed my mind.

"Whoever is behind this could very well be connected with the funeral business," Chase said. "Please be careful around Drew."

"You think . . ." I couldn't even finish my thought. I couldn't say the words out loud. The words: you think Drew could be behind this? I'd pondered them before but had tried to dismiss the thought.

"We don't know anything at this point. And, please, whatever you do, don't tell him. Okay? We need to keep the upper hand here."

"Okay, got it."

"Where are you anyway?"

"At Wilford," I croaked.

Just then, a footstep sounded behind me. "You ready

to go, Holly?"

I dropped my phone when I heard Drew's voice behind me.

***

I turned around, feeling out of sorts.

Embalming fluid.

Used to kill.

Someone connected with the funeral home business.

A secret PO box.

ID theft? Jewelry theft?

I remembered Drew's nice house. His nice clothes. How he valued his reputation.

Could Drew be the killer? Or could he even be covering up for a killer? Maybe he'd asked me out with ulterior motives also. Maybe there weren't any guys out there who liked me for me.

I had to play this carefully. And I needed more information.

Because Drew had been in the shower, he wasn't the man outside.

Unless he was working with someone. Maybe there was an entire network of people involved. Maybe Blake was one of them. Or maybe she was a victim. I had so many questions and uncertainties right now.

"Holly?"

I intended on turning toward him but instead I twirled around, jumpier than I should be if I was going to play this right.

I grabbed my phone from the floor. Chase's voice

still rang through the line, but I hit End anyway, and slid my phone into my purse.

As lightning flashed again, I stepped forward and swung my head toward the door.

The man was gone.

Fear trickled down my throat.

Where had he gone? Was he trying to get inside? Or had he only been trying to scare me?

"Holly?" Drew touched my arm.

I finally looked at him. At kind, considerate Drew, who looked at me now with concern and compassion.

He wasn't involved in this.

I licked my dry lips, trying to pull myself together. "There was someone at the door."

A wrinkle formed between his eyebrows. "Trying to get in?"

I shook my head. "I . . . I don't think so. I think he was trying to send a message."

I couldn't tell Drew that I knew about the formaldehyde. No, I'd just be setting myself up to get killed.

His questioning look was replaced with concern. "You think the man behind these threats is here? Did you call the police?"

I glanced at my phone and nodded. "Yes, I did. They're on their way."

Chase would come here, right? I didn't need to spell it out for him.

Drew touched my arm and pulled me away from the door. "Let's just wait it out until they get here then, okay? No one needs to play hero. All the doors are locked, so we'll be safe inside."

I nodded.

"Let's go back to the lounge area. I can make some coffee until the police arrive."

He led me toward the back. I wasn't sure I should go with him. I wanted to believe in him, but I wanted to be wise.

As we reached the back hallway, I froze and pointed to the floor.

Wet footprints led from the outside door.

Whoever had been outside was now in here.

I could hardly breathe at the thought.

CHAPTER 26

Two seconds after I spotted the footprints, the power went out.

I didn't know whether to jump into Drew's arms or if I should run far from him.

I didn't want to believe he could be behind this, but I couldn't be naïve. My life could be in danger right now.

"Drew . . ." I pointed to the floor.

He turned on the flashlight app on his phone and shined it in the direction I pointed. "Are those . . .?"

"Footprints," I answered. "Someone's in here with us."

He took my arm. "Let's go to my office. Now."

The skin on my neck crawled. There could be a killer in here with us.

Could this get any worse?

Just then, someone pounded on the door.

The killer?

No, he wouldn't knock.

Chase. It was Chase.

"It's probably the police," I rushed, relief pouring through me.

"Come on." He took my hand and pulled me back toward the front of the building. Drew, familiar with the locks, easily opened the front door.

If he was the killer, he wouldn't have done that, right? He would have kept me trapped inside. He would have killed me.

Chase darted out of the downpour. He ignored Drew and came straight to me.

"Are you okay?" He grasped my shoulders, his eyes probing into mine.

I nodded, feeling numb yet overwhelmed, scared yet relieved, confused yet more certain by the moment. "Yeah, I'm fine."

Hesitantly, he seemed to step away. He dropped his hands and scowled as he turned to Drew. "My guys are looking outside."

"There were footsteps leading inside from a side exit," Drew said.

"You two stay here." Chase drew his gun and stepped toward the darkness.

As Chase left, a new thought hit me. What if Drew had stepped outside while he was supposedly taking a shower? His hair was already wet. I wouldn't have been able to tell the difference.

But why would he do that?

My emotions clashed as I stood huddled against the wall . . . with Drew. He was saying something, but I barely heard him.

A few minutes later, Chase reappeared. "I didn't see anyone inside. It looks like they got away before we got here. Could you tell anything about the person?"

"It appeared to be a man," I started, remembering that silhouette. "That was about it. It was so dark."

He turned to Drew. "Did you see anything?"

Drew shook his head. "I was getting cleaned up after work. I wasn't out here for any of it."

"Have you had any trouble with anyone here?" Chase asked. "Any employees?"

Drew shrugged. "I can't say I have. No more than what you already know."

"Okay then," Chase said. "I think you're okay here for the evening. But it would be wise to be cautious until we know what's going on."

"Of course," Drew said.

Chase's gaze lingered on me one more minute. What was he trying to tell me? Had he discovered something else?

"Can I speak with you a minute, Holly?" he asked. "In private."

My throat tightened again.

"I'll give you two a minute," Drew said. His voice sounded indifferent, but his shoulders looked stiff and uptight. "I need to run to my office anyway."

Another round of guilt pounded through me as Drew walked away.

It wasn't fair to him that I doubted his innocence. But I couldn't tell him what I knew. Not yet. I needed more proof—or lack thereof—first.

Chase waited until he was out of earshot before he said, "You gave me a scare."

"I'm sorry," I whispered. "Drew came out, and everything you said was still fresh in my mind. I dropped the phone."

"I'm glad you're okay."

"You really didn't see anyone outside?" I questioned, making sure he wasn't withholding information around Drew.

"I didn't. But I have a feeling this goes deeper than we initially thought."

"Did your analysts discover anything about the jump drive?"

"Not yet. They're working on it as we speak."

"What should I do?" I rubbed my arms, suddenly cold.

He nodded toward Drew's office. "I would stay away from that guy until we know what's going on."

"But if he's innocent . . ." My mind raced through possibilities. However, Chase was not the one to hash out my dating dilemma with.

If I stayed away from Drew because he could be guilty but it turned out he was innocent, then I could put our possible relationship and any future together at risk. But if he was a killer, obviously my actual life was more important than my love life.

"You have some choices to make, Holly."

I nodded. "Yeah, I do."

***

Perhaps it was an unwise choice, but I decided to go to dinner with Drew despite everything I knew. We'd be out in public and safe. And I'd insisted on driving separately. Drew hadn't seemed to mind.

Despite all my logic, I was practically beside myself as I pulled up to Bertie's. Drew and I met in the parking lot, and he escorted me inside. We found a corner table and settled there.

The place was a true hole in the wall. As soon as I saw the outdated but clean space, I figured it would be a winner. When I saw that every waitress was fifty or older, it was confirmed.

I studied Drew as I sat back in my chair. Though we'd been together earlier, I hadn't really gotten a good look at him. He was dressed more casually right now, wearing a T-shirt and jeans. It was actually a nice look. I'd only seen him dressed up—or in scrubs—before. When did Drew not look nice? With his classic features, he could grace *GQ Magazine* easily.

"I'm sorry you had to be there for that earlier," Drew said. "I'm sorry you have to be tangled up in this at all, for that matter."

"I was going to say the same thing to you," I said. "I feel like I'm the one who's pulled you in."

If Drew was telling the truth, he was just as much a victim here as anyone.

But if he was lying, then he was one twisted, devious excuse for a human being.

My thoughts on which one he was volleyed back and forth every few seconds.

The waitress appeared to take our order. I quickly glanced at the menu before picking a waffle with bacon. Healthy eating was out the window right now. I needed comfort food. The more, the merrier.

Drew, on the other hand, got a veggie omelet and

whole wheat toast. I guess he didn't get as fit as he was on accident.

"Is your life always like this?" Drew asked as the waitress walked away.

I shrugged, unsure how to answer. "Maybe."

"Well, I for one hope this is all over soon."

"I hope so also." And, in order for this to be over, I needed to get some answers.

There was only one way I knew to do that.

After a moment of thought, I grabbed my phone. "I know this is going to seem crazy, but do these numbers mean anything to you?"

He stared at my phone for several minutes. I tried to read his expression. Did he recognize the information? I couldn't tell. Or was he honestly perplexed? For once, I didn't have a good read on it.

"There doesn't appear to be much rhyme or reason to them, does there?"

I released my breath, halfway relieved. I only hoped he was being honest. "Not to my knowledge."

He handed my phone back to me. "I wish I could help you out, Holly. I really do. But I have no idea. At first glance, it looked like Social Security numbers that were listed. Is this connected with Travis and Chuck's murders?"

I rubbed my lips together. "Possibly."

"I'm not even going to ask how you got ahold of that information."

"It's better if you don't know," I told him.

"You think this is about the jewelry?"

How much did I say? I wanted to feel him out—

carefully. "I think it goes deeper than that. Maybe ID theft."

He leaned back and stared at the wall behind me for a minute. "So maybe Travis's theft ring ran deeper than jewelry? Maybe it's like you said and he was stealing identities as well."

I wanted to get excited and believe that was true, but I had the feeling that wasn't the case.

Drew swung his head back and forth and shrugged. "It's hard to say what was going on. Travis certainly didn't open up to me."

I didn't want to keep pushing too hard. I needed to be careful how I planned each of my moves here.

A shadow covered our table and I looked up to see the hipster standing there. What was his name? AJ, I thought.

"Hey, man!" Drew said. "What's going on?"

AJ shrugged. "I was just getting a sandwich to go."

"You've been working too hard lately. Hardly time to eat, huh?"

"You could say that." He nodded toward me. "Holly, right?"

"That's right." I smiled.

"Okay, I don't want to interrupt you two. I just saw you over here and wanted to say hello."

"Glad I got to see you before you left," Drew said.

"Yeah, I'm headed to Florida next week," AJ said. "I have the best job ever."

"He gets to go to a conference," Drew explained. "Life Force knows how to pick the perfect locations for their annual meetings."

AJ shrugged. "What can I say? I can't say it enough—I have the best job ever. I just hope this whole fiasco here is cleared up by the time I return. I think all of us have been stressed lately."

"I couldn't agree more," Drew said.

Before I could ask more questions, my phone buzzed. I usually didn't pay attention to my cell while I was with other people, but, for some reason, I took a quick peek to see whom the message was from.

When I looked at the screen, I saw Travis's number. Below it was a picture of Blake with the words "It was supposed to be you" at the bottom.

CHAPTER 27

"I have to go to the police," I muttered, hurrying toward the door.

"I'll go with you." Drew followed me.

"Don't feel like you have to."

"I don't," Drew said. "I want to. Besides, you're in no state to drive."

I thought about showing up at the police station, talking to Chase with Drew in tow. It could be ugly. Non-harmonious. Totally awkward. I didn't want to invoke the same feelings in Chase as he'd invoked in me when I saw that lipstick on his collar.

But Drew was right. I wasn't in a good state to drive.

My muscles stretched so tight that my back ached and my stomach felt ripe to do unpleasant things as I entered the station. Drew kept a hand on my lower back.

Chase stood as I walked into his office. The compassion in his eyes faded as his gaze traveled behind me to Drew. The ultra-professional Chase replaced the kind, intimate one I'd known and halfway expected.

Despite all logic, the realization twisted my gut.

Life was rarely as simple as I longed for it to be. The more relationships I was tangled in, the more complex it seemed to grow.

The two men exchanged courteous nods.

"What's going on?" Chase asked. "It sounded urgent."

"I knew you'd want to see this right away." I handed him my phone.

His countenance grew dark as he looked at the screen. "This is the confirmation we need that something is wrong. I'll put my IT guys on it and see if they can trace anything. Don't get your hopes up."

"I won't."

Chase called someone into the office to run the photo and he chatted a few minutes with his captain in the hallway.

Just as Chase walked back in, Drew's phone beeped. He glanced at his own screen and then stood. "Would you excuse me a minute? It's my brother, and he says it's urgent."

"Of course," I said.

When he left, Chase stared at me, tension shifting awkwardly between us.

"After all we talked about, you're still with him?" Chase whispered. "Have you lost your mind?"

"I'm trying to give him the benefit of doubt."

"I hope this Prince Charming of yours doesn't get you killed."

"Prince Charming?"

He scowled. "I see the way you look at each other."

"Look, I don't know what's going on here, but you're the one who made the decision about our relationship.

Maybe I called it off, but you refused to commit."

His brow furrowed. "Did you want me to lie to you and tell you that I was looking for forever when I can hardly navigate a single week?"

My pulse pounded in my ears as emotions waged within me. Fire rushed through my veins. "What's that mean?"

He leaned close. "It just means I knew it wouldn't be fair to drag you into my life."

"Isn't that what relationships are? Two broken people dealing with each other's brokenness together?" I caught my voice rising and lowered it. Drew's voice echoed in the hallway.

Chase's gaze softened. "You deserve better than what I can give you right now. You deserve someone like Drew."

I crossed my arms, not willing to let him off the hook that easily. "Even if that's true, you have no room to talk."

"What does that mean?" Chase bristled this time.

Did I have to spell it out for him? Apparently, I did. "I saw the lipstick on your collar the other night, Chase."

"Lipstick on my collar? I don't know what you're talking about." He sounded honestly confused.

I let out a mental sigh. "It was bright pink. I'm not sure how you could miss it."

"Maybe it was from when I had to rescue a woman who'd nearly jumped off a bridge and she clung to me so tightly I feared she might take both of us down."

Guilt pounded through me. "Oh."

Silence stretched. So many thoughts clashed in my

head. This had been the most candid conversation we'd had in a long time, and it was way overdue.

Thoughts about how we'd gotten to this place. This awkward place when we'd both been filled with so much warmth at one time. For a moment, I mourned for what I'd lost. For what we'd lost.

"We're going to have to learn to work together, aren't we?" I finally said. "This isn't easy."

"It's not easy. I'm sorry for snapping."

"Me too. Look, Chase. You mean too much to me to let this happen between us. I want to be friends. To be there for each other."

Chase had no one else. Sure, he had a few friends that he might watch the games with at times. But his family was as good as gone. He'd been a part of my family while we'd dated, and I knew he'd appreciated that support system.

"You think we can really do this?" he asked. "Work together? Be friends?"

"I know it's going to be hard, but I think we can. We just have to be willing to talk."

Before Chase could respond, Drew stepped back into the room and slipped his phone into his pocket. "I'm sorry to say, but with the power outage, we're having some problems with our backup generator at the funeral home. We have to make sure the refrigeration is on or . . . well, you don't want to know. I'm sorry to leave you right now, but I do need to handle this."

"I understand."

"Do you want me to drop you off at your car?"

"I'll give her a ride home," Chase said.

Drew paused, as if unsure how to proceed. Finally, I nodded, trying to reassure him that it was okay. Besides, I really did want to stick around and ask Chase more questions.

"Please, go ahead," I said. "I'll be fine. Don't worry about me."

Despite my words, Drew seemed to hesitate. I stood and met him at the door, taking his arm to step into the hallway.

"Really, I'll be fine," I whispered.

"I feel bad leaving you here." His eyes latched onto mine, and I could see the unspoken concern in his gaze.

Concern over my safety? Over the impoliteness of leaving me? Or over me being with Chase? I wasn't sure. Perhaps it was a combination of all those things.

Or he wanted an excuse to catch me alone and kill me.

So many options.

"No need to feel bad," I told him. "I've done this plenty of times before."

That seemed to break the tension, and Drew shook his head, some of the worry leaving his countenance. "That's not something that would normally assure me. Thankfully we've had a conversation about this before."

I squeezed his arm. "I've got this. Thanks for bringing me."

He took a step back and paused. "I'll call you later."

It almost sounded like a question. I decided not to dwell on that now. "That sounds great."

My cheeks heated when I came back into Chase's office. I hoped he hadn't overheard any of that, but I

270

couldn't worry about that now. Honestly, I just had to stop worrying in general and accept this situation for what it was.

"I just got an update on Blake from one of my guys," Chase said.

"Okay. What did you figure out?"

"Her real name is Kari Harling. Her parents died when she was five, and she grew up in foster care."

"Foster care?" That fact swirled in my head.

"There was never any mold in her apartment and, as far as we can tell, she's not a student at any of the local colleges either. She singled you out for some reason, Holly."

"Was there any connection between her and Travis?"

"Not that we discovered yet."

I leaned back and chewed on that. It was going to take me a while before I drew any conclusions. "What's next?" I asked instead.

He shook his head. "We'll probably contact the media, but I need to speak with my captain about it first. He's reviewing the case right now."

"I know she hasn't been truthful, but I'm worried about her, Chase."

"I'm worried about her. But I'm worried about you as well. You were the intended victim, Holly. The question is why."

CHAPTER 28

Even though Travis and I weren't dating, I headed to his memorial service the next day. I had little choice since I'd been awake most of the night, worried about Blake, unsure about Drew, and replaying my conversation with Chase. This case was going to haunt me until I had some answers.

Not even a late-night chat with Jamie had helped me make sense of things.

Who was behind this?

Raul? Jason? Ronald? Blake? . . . Drew?

I stared at the crowd gathered for the memorial. I had a feeling the killer would be here. He was someone who knew Travis, and if he didn't show up, that would seem suspicious. Knowing I was in the room with a killer did little to comfort me.

A decent crowd had shown up, and right now everyone mingled before the service started. There was an overall air of positivity, despite the reason for gathering. Huey Lewis played on the overhead. Apparently, he was Travis's favorite.

The Hookers had already assaulted—I mean

greeted—me, and they acted like our entire conversation earlier this week about how Travis and I weren't dating hadn't happened. And, again, they were grieving, so I had hesitations about setting them straight during this difficult time.

While nestled near the wall, I watched Drew across the room. He was in his element here. The perfect gentleman and host. He made people feel at ease and welcome, and he seemed like a natural.

But he also seemed burdened, I realized, and I didn't know why. Some of his lightness was gone, replaced with stiff movements and a hesitant smile. Had everything caught up with him? Had something new happened? I had no idea, and I hadn't had the opportunity to talk to him alone.

"I'm surprised you'd show your face here," a deep voice said behind me.

I turned and saw Raul. Instantly, I remembered when he'd confronted me earlier, and I scowled. "I could say the same for you."

He stood beside me and crossed his arms. "You don't like me."

"Can you blame me after our last talk?"

He shrugged. "I guess not."

Silence stretched, and I waited for him to get the hint and leave.

"You miss working here?" I asked, deciding to fish for information since he wasn't going anywhere.

"Not on your life. I'm not cut out for this kind of work."

"You probably make better money selling medical

equipment anyway." Maybe money was important to him—important enough to steal from the dead.

His hefty jaw flexed. "It was never about the money. This is an interesting life working here. Living with the dead."

"That's an interesting way to word it."

"It's not for me. Hang around much longer, and you'll see what it's like."

"What do you mean?" I asked.

"I'm talking about the business of death. The business of profiting from other people's heartache. It's not just the funeral home. It's the people who sell caskets and flowers and cemetery plots. I'm not saying these people don't have good hearts. But there's a dark side that people don't see."

I couldn't help but wonder how much this guy knew about stuff around me. Did he have suspicions about anyone in these circles? Maybe people who dealt with death so often were more prone to be desensitized when it came to murder.

I didn't really want to think about the business of death. Those who sold caskets and tombstones and flower arrangements. All those things were needed, but it seemed so uncouth to profit off someone else's loss.

I turned toward him, watching his expression. "Something fishy is going on here at the home. Do you know anything about it?"

His gaze darkened. "No, and if you cause trouble, I'll make sure you get some trouble."

"That sounds like a threat."

"Take it for what you want. I watch out for my

family."

"How far do you take that?" My gaze latched onto his. "Do you lie for them? Set up secret PO boxes?"

"What are you talking about?" He glowered at me.

"I see the two of you have met."

We both turned and saw Drew standing there. Instantly, we cooled.

"I was just going." Raul took a step away—but only after he gave me a warning glance.

"I hope he wasn't giving you a hard time," Drew said. "He can be rough around the edges sometimes."

"No, I'm fine. I've handled worse."

"I'm sure you have." He smiled faintly and came to stand beside me.

I could feel the heaviness surrounding him. Was it because of the funeral? Because he knew Travis? Or was it something else?

"Is everything okay?" I asked.

He seemed melancholy today, which was unlike him.

"I had an interesting talk with someone this morning," he said.

"About what?"

He glanced around and then pulled me toward the corner. "I got a letter this week from someone whose dad received a bone donation. She asked me to forward the letter to the family of the donor—the names aren't usually public. I needed a pick-me-up so I decided to deliver the letter myself in person this morning."

"Okay. That seems like it would brighten your day."

His gaze clouded. "The woman told me that her husband—who died of a heart attack—wasn't a donor."

I blanched at his words. "I'm sure there's a process you go through for this, correct? Maybe, in the midst of her grief, she forgot."

"There's a lot of paperwork that has to be filled out and signed, but I can attest to the fact that her memory wasn't faulty."

"So . . . what happened?"

"That's what I'm trying to figure out. It just doesn't make sense. I came back here and found the paperwork. It had been signed. But I compared that signature to her signature on some other paperwork, and they didn't quite match."

The truth lingered in the back of my mind. It wasn't fully formed yet, but this was the key to this mystery, wasn't it?

Before I could ask more questions, someone called Drew away.

And I had a lot to think about.

***

To my surprise, I saw Chase come in a few minutes later. He joined me at the back of the room. The music had changed from Huey Lewis to Guns N' Roses.

He nodded toward a screen at the front. "I thought you never met this guy face-to-face?"

I looked at a picture of me and Travis with a Caribbean infused sunset behind us. "I didn't. Photoshop."

I couldn't believe the Hookers had used those photos even after I'd told them they weren't real. Now I knew where Travis had learned to be a compulsive liar.

"That's . . . sad." Chase stared at the screen as another photo of Travis and me popped up. This time we were visiting the pyramids.

"Isn't it?" I muttered. "I didn't realize you were coming. And wearing a suit at that."

"I figured it couldn't hurt to come and see if I could find out anything. Maybe to even keep you out of trouble."

"Me?" I asked innocently.

"Yes, you." Chase stood with his hands in pockets, a casual look, but he surveyed the room in a way that was anything but casual. "So, you see any suspects here?"

My mind still turned over what Drew had told me. "I see all of them. I learned something new, Chase."

I told him what Drew told me.

"Now we're getting somewhere," he muttered. "It's finally making sense."

I nodded, still trying to piece everything together. "I agree. Someone is forging those documents and then pocketing the money from the donations. Travis and Chuck must have found out about it. Maybe they were involved, even."

"So, who's the ringleader here?" Chase asked. "Let's hear your theories."

"There are several possibilities. Starting with Ronald Dillow." I nodded across the room to the man as he talked with the Hookers.

"He has an alibi."

"That's true, but I have a feeling there's more than one person involved here." I nodded toward Drew's brother. "Then there's Raul."

"Why is he a suspect?"

"He had some heated conversations with Travis apparently. Someone here also set up that fake PO box. Raul could definitely do that. He had access to this whole place."

"Good to know."

"Then there's Jason. He said he was in Wisconsin, but I saw him in some of the photos taken at the scene the night Travis died."

"I talked to him," Chase said. "He claims he stayed in town because he had a blind date in the area."

"Then why didn't he stick around when he learned his friend had died?"

"He suspected something bad was going down with Travis. That's why he told everyone he was leaving town for a while. He says he wanted to lie low, just in case the killer came looking for him."

"You believed him?" I asked.

"The jury's still out. We did talk to his date, and she said she was with him during the time of the murder."

I bristled as someone new walked in. "And there's Dr. Dan Gilbert. What in the world is he doing here?"

As if he'd heard me, he strode my way.

"You're here," he grumbled.

"I am." I raised my chin. "I could say the same for you."

Chase nudged his way in front of me, and Dr. Gilbert took a step back.

"Listen, I'm not here for trouble," Dan said. "In fact, I should say thanks for that conversation you had with me outside my house. You got me thinking, and I left that night for an intense rehab. I know I need to move past this."

Surprise washed through me. "Really?"

I supposed that was his alibi also.

He nodded. "I was ready to kill you. Like totally ready to blow your brains out. When I realized that, I knew I was out of control."

"I'm . . . glad I could help." I had no idea he'd actually been that close.

"Now I'm going to work on forgiveness. That's why I'm here. I'm going to start with forgiving Travis Hooker."

"Good for you," I said.

Chase leaned toward me as Dr. Gilbert walked away. "You only told me an abbreviated version about your conversation with Dan Gilbert apparently."

I frowned. "I figured you weren't interested in all the details."

He let out a skeptical uh-huh.

"I think you've left off the most obvious suspect," Chase said.

"Who's that?"

He nodded to someone in the distance. "Drew."

My heart twisted. "Drew didn't do this. If he did, why would he tell me about that donor letter?"

"To throw you off his scent."

I shook my head. "I just can't see it."

"Maybe you should open your eyes. Because he's the most obvious suspect here."

CHAPTER 29

All throughout the service, my mind raced as I reviewed the facts.

Travis is dead.

A key is stashed in my pocket.

Blake appears, pretending to be related.

Chuck is dead.

Man breaks into my house and threatens me.

Blake disappears.

Jump drive found with possible invoice numbers, Social Security numbers, and large payment amounts.

Someone desperate to scare me away.

Someone at Wilford has a secret PO box to funnel some kind of correspondence—and possibly money. Possibly connected with these invoices.

Whoever was behind this was in just the right position to coordinate this and know how to profit off this venture. It wouldn't be everyday knowledge.

I had a sneaking suspicion as to who might be guilty. Now I had to figure out how to prove it.

And I had a plan. It might be a horrible plan, but it was all I had right now.

When the service ended, there was a light social immediately afterward. And, by light social, I meant cookies and coffee in the lobby. It was unconventional, apparently, but the funeral home had made an exception since Travis had worked with them.

I grabbed a cup of java, and I waited for my opportunity.

As I took a sip, I looked around. Chase was still here, watching everything.

Drew mingled, taking care of business.

Raul sulked in the background, some kind of chip on his shoulder.

Jason remained, staying in town for long enough to pay his respects—without raising suspicions perhaps.

Ronald acted like he'd never been accused of murdering the man.

The Hookers moved about the crowd, talking to everyone.

Alicia and AJ talked in the corner.

Even Dr. Gilbert was mixing and mingling.

Finally, I saw my opportunity to act. I casually walked across the room, holding my coffee. My bones trembled, which would make what I did next easier and more natural. I hoped.

My shoulder bumped into Ronald Dillow as we crossed paths.

The jolt caused my coffee to fly all over AJ.

He gasped and muttered a few choice words.

Alicia grabbed some napkins and handed them to him.

"I'm so sorry," I rushed. "I just . . . I'm all off-balance.

I hate funerals."

My words seemed to soften him. He still looked put off, but he tried to gain some civility. "It's okay."

"Drew!" I called him over. "Could you show AJ where your shower is? This is all my fault. I accidentally spilled my coffee on him."

Drew joined me and squinted. "Of course. I even have a shirt you can change into."

"You don't have to do that," AJ muttered.

"Of course, we do. This is my fault." I took his arm and began leading him toward the back.

I stole a glance at Chase as we escorted AJ.

I hoped this paid off. I really hoped it paid off because I had no other options. AJ fussed and insisted we didn't have to do this, and I kept insisting that we did and acting flustered.

Drew looked clueless, but he was going with it.

"Here," Drew said, opening a door in the back. "Go ahead and clean up."

AJ looked perturbed as he stepped inside. I waited there. After a few minutes, I cracked the door and saw that AJ was in a stall. Quietly, I snuck inside and grabbed the clothes that he'd draped over the divider there.

"What are you doing, Holly?" Drew asked.

"You'll see."

I didn't repeat myself. Instead, I reached into AJ's pockets. I found one cellphone and clicked on the screen. It looked like it belonged to AJ.

I dug into the other pocket and hit the jackpot. Another cellphone.

I hit the screen and my pulse raced.

It was Travis's. And I bet if I dug through the messages, I'd find some texts that AJ had sent me—some threats.

"What's going on?" Chase joined us, apprehension written on his face.

"AJ killed Travis and Chuck," I said.

A knot formed between Chase's eyes. "Are you sure?"

"What?" Drew asked.

I held up Travis's phone. "It's all right here."

Just then, the door opened, and AJ stuck his head out. "Where are my—"

He paused when he saw us with his phones.

"It's not what it looks like." He backed up, a towel wrapped around his midsection.

Chase bristled. "I think we need to go down to the station and talk."

AJ tried to run but slipped and sprawled on the floor.

Chase pulled him to his feet. "Okay, we'll do this your way."

***

Alicia shook her head. "I can't believe AJ killed Travis and Chuck. You think you know someone . . ."

"He had us all fooled," Drew muttered.

"It didn't make sense until you told me about that donor letter," I said. "The whole time I was focusing on jewelry or IDs. I never thought it could be bones and tissues."

He stared off in the distance. "He must have forged

my name on those forms. He came to pick up the donations from me, but he was somehow pocketing the money from the insurance companies. He must have opened that PO box also as a way to ensure I didn't get any of the invoices or correspondence from Life Force."

"He thought everything through," I said.

"I just can't believe I couldn't see this." He shook his head. "I thought AJ was my friend."

"My guess is that Travis or Chuck discovered what he was doing and threatened to turn him in. Somehow AJ convinced them to come on board instead. He probably gave them a cut. All of that was fine until their consciences started to get to them. They saved the information about AJ's transactions onto that jump drive and made sure I got hold of it."

"Why you?" Alicia asked.

"Travis read an article in the paper about some past crimes I'd solved. He thought he could trust me more than the police."

Alicia wandered away, leaving only Drew and me standing there.

Drew turned toward me, still appearing melancholy. "Good job, Holly."

"Thanks."

He stared at me, an unreadable expression on his face.

"What is it?" I asked.

He pressed his lips together before asking, "Holly, have you been investigating . . . me? Is that what we were all about?"

My heart pounded furiously in my ears. "Of course

not. It wasn't like that."

"Then what was it like?"

"I was trying to prove your innocence, not your guilt." My voice caught.

"But you were using me."

I knew how horrible it felt to be the victim of ulterior motives. I didn't want Drew to feel that way. "No, I wasn't. I had no idea when I met you the turn all of this would take. And then when I realized something was going on . . ."

His gaze pierced into mine. "Then what?"

I swallowed hard, wishing I could erase the hurt from his eyes. "I had to figure out who was behind this, Drew. My life was on the line. So was Blake's, I thought."

He shook his head, looking unconvinced. "I thought we had something special."

"I think we do. Please believe me, Drew. This was never about setting you up."

Drew stepped back. "I'm going to need to think about this for a while."

My heart sank, and I wanted to plead with him. But I knew he needed space. In a few days, he might reconsider. "I understand. Of course."

He nodded, opened his mouth as if he wanted to say something else, and then stepped back. He didn't say goodbye or anything else. He just walked away.

I closed my eyes, hating the emotions churning inside me.

I'd solved a crime but ruined a relationship, and that wasn't okay.

CHAPTER 30

That evening, I went to Jamie's house and rehashed everything with her.

"Oh, girl," she muttered. "What are you going to do?"

My heart felt heavier than I thought it would, considering I'd solved the case. "What should I do?"

"I have no idea. I'm glad you didn't fall in love with a serial killer."

I made a face. "Me too."

"What about Blake?"

"Chase said they're questioning AJ, hoping to get the information out of him."

"Hopefully they'll find her soon."

I wrapped my arms over my chest. "I hope so."

Part of me was heartbroken over the fact that Drew felt like I'd betrayed him.

Part of me still thought about Chase. But I was quick to remind myself that we had no future together. I had to keep that in the forefront of my mind.

My phone buzzed, and I glanced down at the screen. It was Drew.

Drew: **I've been thinking. Can we talk?**

My pulse spiked.

Me: **Of course. Name the place.**

Drew: **Could you swing by the funeral home? I'm wrapping things up here now.**

Me: **Absolutely. I'll be there in 10 minutes.**

"Drew wants to meet," I told Jamie.

"Oh . . . maybe he's finally come to his senses."

"Maybe. At least I'll know one way or the other where we stand with each other."

"You still sound torn."

I sighed. "I guess I am. But feeling torn doesn't mean I should be indecisive."

"Girlfriend, that's true. Let me know how it goes."

"Hopefully the fact that we're talking at the funeral home won't be a death wish."

"You're funny, girl. I'll be praying for you. I know stuff like this stresses you out."

I told her goodbye and grabbed my purse. I didn't know what this conversation could lead to. But at least I'd have some closure. There was a lot to be said for that.

For a moment—and just a moment—I hesitated, wondering how safe this was. Then I remembered that AJ was locked up. This was all over.

Fifteen minutes later, I pulled up to the funeral home. I never in a million years thought I'd willingly spend so much time at a funeral home. Thankfully, Drew's Mustang was out front. That eased the tension stretching through me.

I just needed to get this conversation over with.

The front door was unlocked, so I stepped inside.

Unfortunately, it was dark in the lobby, which didn't do anything for my nerve factor.

I swallowed, my throat achy, as I glanced around, searching for Drew. Or even a light that was on.

Faint illumination crept through a hallway in the back. That must be where he was.

"Drew said he's waiting for you," someone said.

I nearly jumped out of my skin. Alicia appeared from the back, an apologetic grin on her face.

"Sorry, I didn't mean to frighten you," she said.

"I didn't hear you coming."

She nodded toward the door. "I'm just leaving actually. We're wrapping up a last-minute request."

"Last minute, huh?"

"They're the worst. Almost the most painful to deal with, but we try to accommodate, just for decency's sake."

I shivered for some reason. "I understand."

She paused near me. "By the way, thanks for listening the other night. I didn't know who else to go to about that PO box."

"I'm glad I could help. I'm just sorry all this happened to all the good people who worked here. I know AJ was your friend."

"You just never know about some people." She pulled her purse up higher on her shoulder. "Well, I'll let you and Drew talk."

"Thanks, Alicia."

"Have a good night, Holly."

Drawing in a shaky breath, I started down the hallway. I really wished I'd asked Alicia to flip on some lights. But I hadn't. The good news was that the bad guy was behind bars.

"Hello?" I called, hoping that Drew might emerge, and I wouldn't have to go any farther into the building. This was all too creepy for me.

He didn't respond.

I pushed my apprehension down and continued along the hallway. Finally, I heard a faint music playing from one of the rooms.

Was that Bing Crosby?

Well, there was always Bing. He made everything better.

I knocked at the door before stepping inside. "Drew?"

I scanned the room. It was the crematory. Of course. It *had* to be the crematory.

He didn't respond, so I took another step. "Hello?"

Maybe he was changing or taking a shower?

But as I rounded the door, I spotted Drew. He was tied to a chair with tape strapped over his mouth.

CHAPTER 31

"Drew!" I started toward him when I heard something behind me. A footstep. Movement.

"I wouldn't do that if I were you," someone said.

I froze and slowly turned. Alicia. She hadn't left. She'd followed me back here, and she was now holding a gun.

All the moisture left my throat. "Alicia, what are you doing? I thought you were leaving."

"I had a few loose ends to wrap up," she said with a snarl.

Gone was the sweet girl next door and, in her place, was a conniving killer. She'd had me fooled. She'd had a lot of people fooled.

"I bet you didn't know when I talked about a last-minute project that I was talking about you, Holly."

I thought about the crematory and everything that Drew had told me about that process, and all the moisture left my throat. Was she planning on making me live my final minutes in that oven? This wasn't good.

"Let's not be irrational here," I said, slowly backing away from her.

CHRISTY BARRITT

"I'm not irrational." Anger flashed in her eyes. "In fact, I'm very rational. Do I make myself clear?"

"Of course." The last thing I wanted was to agitate her further. No, I needed to keep her calm. "What do you want me to do?"

"Climb up there." Using her gun, she pointed to the gurney where a wooden coffin usually sat before being pushed into the flames.

"No," I said. She was going to have to shoot me first.

"Get up there or I'm going to shoot your little boyfriend."

I glanced at Drew. His eyes were wide, and he shook his head, making it clear he didn't want me to listen to Alicia.

I stepped closer to Drew. "You're not going to get away with this, Alicia."

"Of course, I am. I have everything planned out."

"Why are you even doing this? AJ is behind bars. You're free and clear."

She sneered again. "The police will realize soon enough that he's only a minion in this. He did what I asked him to do and turned a blind eye to everything else. They'll realize it was me who was behind it. I'm the only one who could have forged that information. Me or Drew. I'm going to point this back to Drew."

My gaze went to her gun again. Her hands didn't even tremble. She had no qualms about this, did she? "How are you going to explain how both Drew and I are dead? The police are going to figure out that you're behind this. It's just a matter of time."

"You underestimate me."

"How so? How will they think Drew is responsible?"

"I used his name on all the correspondence I've been feeding through the PO box. I've also put some cash deposits into a safety deposit box, also in his name." Her eyes glimmered with satisfaction.

"You take a lot of pride in that, don't you?" I asked, my gaze searching the room for something I could use. I saw a tray of equipment in the distance. Was there a scalpel there? Even if there was, Alicia would shoot me before I could reach it.

The satisfaction in her gaze deepened. "Of course."

"But that's still not going to explain my death."

"Of course it is. I did research on you. I know how nosy you are. You caught on to what Drew was doing. He felt threatened, so he got rid of you."

I glanced at Drew. "And Drew? What happens to him?"

"I'll dispose of his body, but I'm going to clean up his remains. Maybe scatter them into the Ohio. I've already purchased a ticket to the Caribbean in his name. Everyone will think he ran."

"No one who knows him will think that." I eyeballed that scalpel. If only . . .

Her eyes narrowed. "Everyone has a dark side."

"Especially you, huh?"

She stepped closer, that gun still pointed at me. "My dad was a mortician. I know all about this stuff. There's no reason for people to be selfish. After they're dead, why does it matter if they have all their organs or tissues or bones? It doesn't."

"I understand."

"My brother died because he couldn't find a match." Her voice lowered to a bitter-sounding growl. "All he needed was a new heart, but no one wanted to give theirs up. They should have to. There shouldn't be a choice."

"I can only imagine how that made you feel. But this isn't the way to solve the problem."

I backed up, almost all the way to Drew now. I could feel his eyes on me.

"I'm in too deep now," Alicia said. "I have no other choice."

She raised her gun.

I put my hands in the air, desperate to buy some time. "You always have a choice."

She twitched, as if battling inside herself. "You don't know what you're talking about. I need to end this. Now. So, get up there, and let's start this process."

"You're going to have to shoot me first, Alicia. No way am I purposefully being burned alive. You're crazy."

"Then I shoot him." She swung the gun toward Drew.

"You're not thinking this through, Alicia." Sweat trickled down my back.

"I'm done thinking things through. Let's get this over with."

"No."

"Take the tape off his mouth," she ordered. "Let's make this a three way conversation. I want to hear what Mr. and Mrs. Perfect here have to say before they meet their demise."

I reached toward Drew and grabbed the end of the silver duct tape. I mouthed "I'm sorry" before ripping the tape from his lips. He blanched and shook his head, but his discomfort only lasted a minute.

"Don't do this, Holly," he said, his voice raspy with emotion. "I'm sorry you've been pulled into this."

"There." Alicia sneered, stepping closer and glowering at us. "You've talked. Now let's get this over with. There's no need to delay the inevitable."

She walked closer, until the gun was only inches from my head.

"Alicia, you can stop this now," Drew said. "This isn't you."

"Of course, this is me! I got in too deep, and now this is the only way out. One tissue donor can help fifty people. Do you know what that means? It means that I helped almost six hundred people through what I did. Six hundred people now have better lives because of me, but most people will never see it. They'll only see me as a monster." Her eyes misted.

If I was going to make a move, it had to be soon.

Before I could, my cell phone rang.

The sound caused Alicia to gasp. As she did, Drew swung the chair around. The legs collided with her and sent her toppling to the floor. Her gun clattered onto the tile.

We both lunged for it at the same time.

I knew whoever got the weapon first, would be the winner here. The stakes were life or death.

CHAPTER 32

Before either of us could get the gun, a new voice sounded in the room.

"Freeze! Put your hands up!"

I glanced up and saw Chase. He was here.

He kicked the gun away so neither Alicia nor I could grab it. Then he jerked Alicia up and began reading her rights.

For a moment—a split second—I was torn. Run to Chase or run to Drew?

With Chase being occupied, I had my answer. I rushed over to Drew and knelt in front of him. "Are you okay?"

He nodded, even though blood trickled from his forehead. "Yeah, I'm okay. You?"

My hands trembled as I untied him. "I'm alive."

"That's a start."

"I'm glad you're okay," I whispered, finally getting the binding around his wrists undone.

He stretched his arms before helping me with the ties around his ankles. "Good work, Holly. I knew you were tough, but you're even tougher than I thought."

"I've had some experience."

He released his final bind and stood. "Let's not ever do that again."

"I'm good with that."

He pulled me into a quick but hearty hug.

I felt someone behind me and reluctantly let go of Drew.

Chase stood there.

My heart pounded in my ears as I turned toward him. "How'd you know to come here?"

"Thanks to AJ, we were able to find Kari. She told us that Alicia was involved. When I couldn't get in touch with you, I called Jamie. She told me you'd come here, and I feared something might be going on."

"Thank goodness, you came."

"Although it looked like you were handling yourself pretty well." He glanced at Drew. "Both of you."

"I think I'll stick to my day job," Drew said.

"It looks like Alicia was the mastermind behind all of this," Chase said. "AJ was just doing what she told him to do while taking a cut in all this. He was the one who tried to steal your purse and who sent you those texts. Alicia told him what to say, however. The two of them were tailing you together, apparently."

"What about the pawnshop video?"

"Alicia wore a wig, hoping to throw us off her trail. She didn't take that last set of jewelry in until Travis was already dead, and she knew you were looking into things."

"So Blake—Kari—was never involved in this?" I asked.

He shook his head. "It doesn't appear so."

"That's good to know."

"There's one other thing you should know, Holly," Chase said. "I got Kari's DNA results back."

I'd found a piece of gum she left in the trash and given it to Chase, along with a swab of my own DNA. I hadn't thought about it much since I found out she was a fraud. "And . . .?"

Chase stared at me another moment. "They show you and Kari share some kind of family relation."

"What?" That was the last thing I expected to hear.

He nodded. "I can't tell you anymore. That's for you to figure out. But she had nothing to do with this. She just happened to be in the wrong place at the wrong time. It's up to you to figure out if you want to press charges."

"Did you ask her about it when you rescued her?"

"That's the other thing. We found her and took her to the hospital. She somehow managed to slip past the officers there. We don't know where she is."

My stomach sank. So much for getting more answers.

"We'll keep looking for her," Chase said.

"Thank you."

Chase's gaze lingered on Drew a moment before he clamped down and offered a slight nod.

"Take care of her," Chase's voice sounded strained and tight.

Drew offered the same expression in return, his hand tightening at my waist. "I will."

My heart lurched into my throat as Chase turned to

take care of business.

Chase had given his blessings, a fact that filled me with gratitude.

I looked up at Drew and smiled, thankful for new opportunities, new connections, new possibilities.

But this was only the beginning. I still had to figure out how Blake—or Kari, I should say—was related to me. I had no idea what to expect. Literally, no earthly idea.

I only knew the future was somehow looking brighter . . . and even a little more mysterious. And that seemed like something I could definitely embrace.

###

If you enjoyed this book, you may also enjoy these Holly Anna Paladin Mysteries:

Random Acts of Murder (Book 1)
When Holly Anna Paladin is given a year to live, she embraces her final days doing what she loves most—random acts of kindness. But one of her extreme good deeds goes horribly wrong, implicating her in a string of murders. Holly is suddenly thrust into a different kind of fight for her life. Could it also be random that the detective assigned to the case is her old high school crush and present-day nemesis? Will Holly find the killer before he ruins what is left of her life? Or will she spend her final days alone and behind bars?

Random Acts of Deceit (Book 2)
"Break up with Chase Dexter, or I'll kill him." Holly Anna Paladin never expected such a gut-wrenching ultimatum. With home invasions, hidden cameras, and bomb threats, Holly must make some serious choices. Whatever she decides, the consequences will either break her heart or break her soul. She tries to match wits with the Shadow Man, but the more she fights, the deeper she's drawn into the perilous situation. With her sister's wedding problems and the riots in the city, Holly has nearly reached her breaking point. She must stop this mystery man before someone she loves dies. But the deceit is threatening to pull her under . . . six feet under.

Random Acts of Murder (Book 3)

When Holly Anna Paladin's boyfriend, police detective Chase Dexter, says he's leaving for two weeks and can't give any details, she wants to trust him. But when she discovers Chase may be involved in some unwise and dangerous pursuits, she's compelled to intervene. Holly gets a run for her money as she's swept into the world of horseracing. The stakes turn deadly when a dead body surfaces and suspicion is cast on Chase. At every turn, more trouble emerges, making Holly question what she holds true about her relationship and her future. Just when she thinks she's on the homestretch, a dark horse arises. Holly might lose everything in a nail-biting fight to the finish.

Random Acts of Scrooge (Book 3.5)

Christmas is supposed to be the most wonderful time of the year, but a real-life Scrooge is threatening to ruin the season's good will. Holly Anna Paladin can't wait to celebrate Christmas with family and friends. She loves everything about the season—celebrating the birth of Jesus, singing carols, and baking Christmas treats, just to name a few. But when a local family needs help, how can she say no? Holly's community has come together to help raise funds to save the home of Greg and Babette Sullivan, but a Bah-Humburgler has snatched the canisters of cash. Holly and her boyfriend, police detective Chase Dexter, team up to catch the Christmas crook. Will they succeed in collecting enough cash to cover the Sullivans' overdue bills? Or will someone succeed in ruining Christmas for all those involved?

Complete Book List

Squeaky Clean Mysteries
Hazardous Duty
Suspicious Minds
It Came Upon a Midnight Crime
Organized Grime
Dirty Deeds
The Scum of All Fears
To Love, Honor, and perish
Mucky Streak
While You Were Sweeping (A Riley Thomas Novella)
Foul Play
Broom and Gloom
Dust and Obey
Thrill Squeaker
Swept Away
Cunning Attractions
Clean Getaway (coming soon)

Holly Anna Paladin Mysteries
Random Acts of Murder
Random Acts of Deceit
Random Acts of Malice
Random Acts of Scrooge
Random Acts of Greed
Random Acts of Fraud

The Sierra Files
Pounced
Hunted
Pranced
Rattled
Caged (coming soon)

The Worst Detective Ever
Ready to Fumble
Reign of Error
Safety in Blunders
Join the Flub (coming soon)
Blooper Freak (coming soon)

Suburban Sleuth Mysteries
Death of a Couch Potato's Wife

Cape Thomas Series
Dubiosity
Disillusioned
Distorted

Carolina Moon Series
Home Before Dark
Gone By Dark
Wait Until Dark
Light the Dark

Tween Novels
The Curtain Call Caper
The Disappearing Dog Dilemma

The Bungled Bike Burglaries

Stand Alone Novels
The Trouble With Perfect
The Good Girl

Non Fiction Titles
The Novel In Me
Changed

ABOUT THE AUTHOR

USA Today has called Christy Barritt's books "scary, funny, passionate, and quirky."

A *Publishers Weekly* bestselling author, Christy writes both mystery and romantic suspense novels that are clean with underlying messages of faith. Her books have won the Daphne du Maurier Award for Excellence in Suspense and Mystery, have been twice nominated for the Romantic Times Reviewers' Choice Award, and have finaled for both a Carol Award and *Foreword Reviews* magazine's Book of the Year.

She is married to her prince charming, a man who thinks she's hilarious—but only when she's not trying to be. Christy is a self-proclaimed klutz, an avid music lover who's known for spontaneously bursting into song, and a road-trip aficionado.

When she's not working or spending time with her family, she enjoys singing, playing the guitar, and exploring small, unsuspecting towns where people have no idea how accident prone she is.

Find Christy online at:
www.christybarritt.com
www.facebook.com/christybarritt
www.twitter.com/cbarritt

Sign up for Christy's newsletter to get information on all of her latest releases here: www.christybarritt.com/newsletter-sign-up/

If you enjoyed this book, please consider leaving a review.

Made in the USA
Las Vegas, NV
25 July 2024

92883860R00178